After five years' separation from her husband Elliott, Cassie was just about getting over it, and settled happily in Provence, when Elliott turned up again —as her boss. And any idea that her feelings for him were dead was soon dispelled. But he had Michèle Durand now . . .

PRINCE
OF DARKNESS

BY
SUSANNA FIRTH

MILLS & BOON LIMITED
17–79 FOLEY STREET
LONDON W1A 1DR

First published 1979
Australian copyright 1979
Philippine copyright 1979
This edition 1979

© Susanna Firth 1979

ISBN 0 263 73158 8

Set in Linotype Baskerville 10 on 11 pt.

Made and printed in Great Britain by Richard Clay (The Chaucer Press), Ltd., Bungay, Suffolk

CHAPTER ONE

'No, that certainly won't do. It's really nothing out-standing, considering the price you're asking. Rather ordinary, really. Not at all what we're looking for.'

Cassie sighed wearily as, for the umpteenth time that day, she mopped her brow and impatiently pushed back the lock of auburn hair that would persist in falling into her eyes. She was beginning to suspect that the day's outing was in the nature of a joyride for Mr and Mrs Clarke. This was the seventh house she had shown them today and all had been found unsuitable on the flimsiest of excuses despite a lengthy inspection of each one. Mr Thompson had warned her about people who would happily spend their holidays inspecting pro-perties which they had no intention of buying. If that was their idea of fun, dragging round from house to house in the blazing discomfort of the Provençal sun, it certainly wasn't Cassie's, and it was an effort to pin on her bright professional smile and suggest that her clients might like to see somewhere else.

'No, I don't think so.' Mrs Clarke was a faded-looking woman whose mousy exterior was more than compen-sated for by her strident, complaining manner. 'Come along, Harry. I think we've seen quite enough.' She set off down the path to the waiting car, leaving Cassie to secure the door and take the keys. Her words floated back as she went. 'It was ridiculous to send a young girl like that with us. After all, what does she know?' As Cassie caught up with them the older woman addressed her in a patronising tone, glancing pointedly at her left hand which was bare of rings. 'If you had a husband of your own, my dear, you might be able to understand a little more about the sort of house a married couple needs.'

'I expect so,' Cassie agreed levelly, holding on to her temper with effort and feeling the smile freeze on her face as she ushered the couple into the car, climbed into the driver's seat, and prepared to take the Clarkes back to the comfort of their air-conditioned hotel. A husband of her own. If only they knew! If she told them that she was a married woman of over five years' standing, would she have the satisfaction of hearing Mrs Clarke eat her words? She doubted it somehow. Besides, what was the use of assuming the status of a wife when your marriage was an empty nothing and some time soon, when you had plucked up enough courage to take that final step, you were heading for the divorce courts to ensure that the worst mistake you ever made in your life was legally cancelled out and the slate wiped clean.

That was an illusion, if anything was, she thought bitterly, as she started the car and drove carefully along the winding country road which took them from the coast inland to Arles, passing on the way the sturdily constructed farmhouses, squarely set amid the salt flat landscape, cracked now by the summer heat and the drought, which had been worse this year than ever before. It wasn't possible to scrub away the memories and start a new life emotionally unbattered by what had gone before. And how did you put aside the thoughts of the happier times before it had all gone sour?

She smiled ruefully. Besides, Elliott wasn't the sort of man you could dismiss easily. Even now, after all this time apart from him, she could recall as clearly as if he was sitting beside her the lines of that strong, decisive face, the jet-dark eyes that could hold mystery as well as smouldering passion, the slightly cruel lips that offered a sensual promise that Cassie had never been able to resist.

She had recognised that attraction for herself from the very first time she laid eyes on him at a reception in a fashionable Mayfair house, owned by Sir John Stephens, a business associate of her father. Cassie had attended under protest, hating the sort of shallow people who were usually present at such gatherings and the sort of artificial chit-chat that they exchanged. It all held little fascination for her and although she circulated dutifully, smiling and talking to people she knew, she was counting the minutes until she could make her retreat and not seem rude in doing so.

It was then that she glimpsed Elliott's tall, broad-shouldered figure by the door. Immaculately tailored in an evening suit that accentuated his dark, almost swarthy, good looks, he was standing somewhat apart from the other guests, almost as if he realised that he was clearly out of place among this fashionable throng. Obviously he was as bored as she was with the evening's entertainment and making less effort to conceal the fact. The alert, dark features registered an impatience and eagerness to be away. He was so evidently a man of action, unused to mouthing polite nothings and contemptuous of those who did.

'Who is he?' Cassie asked a nearby girl friend. Tania might be an irritating companion at times with her non-stop gossip about her contacts with the famous and the not-so-famous, but if anyone could identify the dark stranger it would be her.

'Gorgeous, isn't he?' Tania sighed wistfully. '*That* is Elliott Grant, the man everyone's tipping to be the next big name in the business world. He started life as a bright protégé of Sir John Stephens, hence his presence here tonight, but he's going places on his own.'

'On his own?' Cassie probed gently.

'Stop fishing!' Tania laughed. 'No, he's not married yet, although he's had his pick of all the eligible women around. Too darned choosy if you ask me, although with those looks as well as brains I suppose he can call the tune. Thinking of trying your luck with him?'

'I might,' Cassie said casually, knowing for certain that she would.

'Then watch your step. He's dynamite and he knows it. If he doesn't like the look of you you'll get an instant brush-off. He doesn't believe in wasting time.'

'That sounds like the voice of experience!'

Her friend shrugged. 'So he didn't fancy me—that's his hard luck. Lots more fish in the sea, even if they don't have his advantages. Good luck with him.' Tania moved away to join a laughing group of young people, leaving Cassie to make her own assault on Elliott Grant.

'Hello. I'm Cassandra Russell, Cassie to my friends.' Even to her own ears the words sounded false and over bright.

It seemed as if he thought so too, for the glance he turned on her was one of bored indifference. For once in her life Cassie expected a rebuff. But she made the effort anyway and went on talking to him, drawn to him as she had never been attracted to any man before, strangely conscious that *this* man was going to be important in her life—why, she did not know.

She was aware of his dark glance raking over her, assessing her quickly and then as swiftly deciding that she was worthy of his attention. She knew she was attractive. She had been praised often enough to her face by ardent male admirers to realise that her pale, delicate features and unusually dark eyes, offset by that flaming aureole of hair, had a rare beauty that could strike the most indifferent man off balance. And Elliott

Grant was not a man to be indifferent where women were concerned.

He had thought her as worthless as the rest of the crowd at first, of that she was sure, a pretty package with a pin-sized brain who might serve to divert his attention from an otherwise boring evening. She fought hard to correct that initial impression and was delighted when she heard him concede after a hotly-contested political argument, 'You're not just a pretty face, are you?'

'Not even,' she countered laughingly, expecting to be contradicted. 'Red hair isn't everyone's idea of female beauty.'

He reached out a hand and stroked the burnished softness and a thrill went through her at his touch. '*I* like it,' he said, as if that was all that mattered and the compliment, if it was intended as such, pleased her more than any she had ever received. He glanced impatiently round. 'I've had enough of this,' he told her. 'We'll get out of this scrum and find somewhere quieter.'

Taking her assent for granted, he found her coat and ushered her from the house to a small Italian restaurant where he was obviously well known. They were left discreetly alone as they ate and then lingered until the early hours drinking coffee and talking about everything under the sun. At the end of that first meeting, when he had driven her home in the black Porsche that was the only sign of ostentation about him, and had kissed her with an expertise that had left her weak and pliant in his arms, she had known that he was the only man for her.

It seemed that he was equally swift at making up his mind. Only a whirlwind two months after they had first met he asked her to marry him, and she accepted without hesitation. Her parents were less enthusiastic about the match. Cassie was their only child, cherished and cocooned, and they could hardly believe that at twenty she was sure enough of her own mind to be ready to leave them, least of all for a man like Elliott.

'After all, he has no background to speak of,' Mrs Russell pointed out carefully. 'And you're so young, so sheltered, Cassie. He's hardly what you're used to, dear.'

'You mean you'd rather I married any one of the suitable young men that you've been slinging at me ever since I left school?' Cassie asked.

'Yes, frankly I would. Believe me, I know his sort,' her father joined the battle. 'You're taking on more than you can handle there. You'll never hold a man like that, Cassie. What can you offer an experienced man beyond your youth and your innocence? He'll be bored with you before the year's out.'

'I don't think so,' Cassie said defiantly. 'He loves me, and he admits that he's never said that to anyone before. And he didn't ask the other women in his life to marry him either!'

In the end Cassie's passionate arguments and belief in Elliott had won the day and, with her parents' reluctant consent, she had married him. But then the problems began. At first she welcomed the thrill of keeping house for the two of them in the small flat that Elliott had bought in a fashionable area of London. She spent the days cleaning the already spotless rooms and trying out new recipes with which to tempt Elliott when he arrived home from his office in the City. The nights when his passionate lovemaking guided her to absolute fulfilment as a woman were as near heaven as she could have imagined. But, when the demands of Elliott's burgeoning career in the high-powered world of the City took more and more of his time and energy, life dragged for her and the arguments started. Accustomed as she was to doting parents who indulged her, it was a new experience for her to come up against someone who refused to give in to her.

'My job's important to me,' Elliott told her firmly. 'I can't just drop everything and rush home, because you're bored and can't manage to amuse yourself for a few hours. Get a job, if you've too much time on your hands. I know your parents would never let you go out to work, but I've no objection, if it'll make you any happier.'

'I'm not trained for anything.'

'Well, go out and get some training. It's about time you stopped assuming that the world owes you a living and saw a little of the real world out there.'

'I don't want a job,' she told him.

'So what do you want? Do you know?' he sounded exasperated.

'You make me sound like a spoilt bitch who doesn't know her own mind. It's not like that,' she protested.

'Isn't it?' he asked roughly. 'It sounds suspiciously like it to me. I warned you how it would be. You walked into this marriage with your eyes wide open. Your parents, to give them credit, had their doubts as to whether it would work. But you married me anyway.'

'I didn't hear you voicing any objections,' Cassie flashed.

'I wanted you,' he said crudely. 'I still do. Physically you stir me up in a way no woman's succeeded in doing before. But if you married me thinking you could change me, mould me more to your liking, you've got another think coming. You married a man with a mind of his own, Cassandra. I'm not prepared to change my life to suit your every whim. I'm not ready to abandon business deals just to take you out when you feel the need for my company. If you wanted some idle, rich dilettante who had time to dance attendance on you all

the hours of the day, you should have settled on someone else.'

'I almost wish I had!' she shouted at him, and he had
stormed out of the flat, slamming the door behind him.

It didn't take her long to discover that Elliott had a
temper to match her own and, as the weeks went by
and the differences between them grew, he became less
and less inclined to keep a check on it. At times she
wondered if he regretted his marriage and was wishing
he had his freedom again. After all, he had played the
field for years. Perhaps he was finding it hard to settle
down with just one woman.

Cassie tried hard to curb her feelings and, for a
while at least, they papered over the cracks. She went to
day classes to learn shorthand and typing and, when she
had achieved a reasonable standard, looked for a job.
But her initial enthusiasm was quelled when she confided in her mother and Mrs Russell had asked with
faint amusement, 'Surely a young bride is too taken up
with her husband so soon after marriage to be looking
to be working for a living when she's no need to? Is
anything wrong between you, dear?'

'No, nothing's wrong,' Cassie had denied hastily, reluctant to confess that there were any problems. 'Everything's fine.'

The quarrels continued, often over nothing at all.
At first they patched up their differences, usually when
Elliott tired of the argument and carried her off to the
bedroom. He made love to her until the memory of
what had caused the dispute between them had been
cast aside, forgotten in their need of each other. Physically she had always been able to satisfy him, an eager
pupil from the first who had turned into a willing
partner. But even in that area of their life it seemed he
had begun to find her inadequate.

'Don't make the mistake of thinking you're the only

woman who can fill my bed satisfactorily,' he taunted her cruelly during the last, bitter row, the culmination of all the arguments they had had during the first months of their marriage.

'In that case you won't miss me when I'm gone, will you?' she asked as she stormed into the bedroom, took down her suitcase from the top of the wardrobe and began to fling her possessions into it in an untidy heap. 'I've had enough, Elliott, do you hear? I'm leaving you and——'

'Going home to Mummy?' he said scathingly. 'That's typical of you. The minute you can't have your own way in something you abandon the fight and run to hide behind your mother's skirts. Why don't you grow up?'

'You never did like my parents, did you? I suppose you resent the fact that I grew up with a stable, secure background, while you——' She paused, suddenly aware that she was hitting below the belt.

'Well, go on. Say it,' he prompted her roughly. 'I wondered when we'd get on to this. Don't mince words. You're the product of rich, doting parents who indulged your every whim, while I was brought up in an orphanage, because my mother couldn't cope with the strain of bringing up a child on her own after my father walked out on her. She wasn't prepared to sign me away for adoption and let someone else do her work for her, so there I stayed until I was old enough to go out and earn my own living.'

'There's no need to throw it in my face as if it was my fault,' Cassie snapped furiously. 'You had a rotten childhood and I'm sorry for you. But does saying I'm sorry make things any better for you?'

'I wasn't asking for your sympathy,' he retorted. 'I'd get precious little if I did. Don't worry, I've always known the score. I was well aware that I wasn't worthy to marry the great Cassandra Russell.'

'It's hardly my fault it you've a chip on your shoulder about the way you started life. It never made a scrap of difference to me,' Cassie said, and meant it.

'Not at first, perhaps. But I wondered how long it would be before you had your doubts and your mother started encouraging them.'

'What do you mean?' In this mood Elliott was impossible to reason with, but she tried nevertheless.

He laughed shortly. 'Your mother made it abundantly clear the first time I met her that she didn't like me as a husband for you. Unfortunately I was what you claimed you wanted and she wasn't used to refusing you anything, was she?'

She felt sick at the sound of the cruel note in his voice. 'I don't have to listen to you any more, Elliott,' she told him as she wrenched open drawers and took out her clothes. 'And I don't intend to. Our marriage was a mistake—that appears to be something we both agree on. There's no more to be said.'

He leaned against the door jamb, outwardly casual, but as deeply moved as she. The dangerous attraction that came from him was as potent as ever. Her senses stirred in spite of herself as she looked at him and she was conscious of another voice within her telling her to back down, now, before it was too late. But he was speaking again and it was already too late, Cassie knew it.

'If you walk out on me, you needn't think I'll follow you and crawl to you to come back to me. I'll find someone to take your place easily enough.'

The words caught her on the raw and she blazed back at him, as furious as he. 'At least it'll make a change for *you* to be looking for company! I'm usually the one who has to do that.'

He took a sudden step towards her, his face dark with

anger and suspicion. 'And what exactly do you mean by that remark?'

In a saner moment Cassie might have drawn back from the brink. But not for nothing did she have a mane of fiery, red-gold hair and a temper to match it, and some demon drove her on. She laughed and asked him carelessly, 'Isn't it obvious? You were never around when I needed you, were you? You were always at the office working late on something. Or should I say someone? It's hardly surprising if I looked elsewhere, is it?'

If she hoped to make him jealous with that taunt, it seemed she had failed.

'I see. Then there's no more to be said, is there?' There was a curiously white look about his mouth as if the strain of keeping his hands off her was suddenly too much for him. 'Don't let me keep you from your packing.' He turned abruptly and left her. From the sitting room came the sound of the drinks cupboard opening and the clink of a glass. Obviously he was seeking consolation in a stiff drink. She wished she could do the same.

Her case packed and the locks secured, Cassie paused irresolutely, her anger ebbing away. How could she have said such things? She hadn't meant them, but when she lost her temper she was capable of saying a lot of things she did not mean. With some idea of making the peace forming in her mind she stepped uncertainly through the door that led to the sitting room.

Elliott was sitting sprawled in an armchair, a glass in his hand and a bottle of whisky on the table beside him.

'Ready to leave?' He put the glass down with a bang that sounded unnaturally loud in the confined space of the room. 'Shall I get you a taxi or are you going to ring home and ask Mummy to send the chauffeur round for you?'

It was obvious that he had no intention of backing

down. Why should she make the first move? And with a hot pride that she had cursed endlessly in the months since, she turned, picked up her case and said coolly and deliberately, 'Neither, Elliott. I'll walk. I need some clean, fresh air after the stale atmosphere in here.'

He shrugged. 'As you please. Goodbye, Cassandra.'

It was strange that he alone never shortened her name, claiming it suited her the way it was. 'Fiery, passionate and never taken seriously,' he had told her, and she had laughed then. In a daze she lifted the suitcase and walked to the door, ignoring his outstretched hand. She was reluctant to say the words that would mean the end of everything between them. Instead she told him, 'I couldn't manage everything. I've had to leave——'

'Collect them some time. I don't want them,' he said curtly.

He might just as well have said that he would prefer all traces of her presence in his life to be eradicated. She winced slightly, but pride forced her on. 'Yes, I'll do that.' She paused, still looking at him. Why did just the sight of him make her stomach turn to jelly and her whole being tremble with desire for him?

'If you're going, get out now.'

If she was going. Did he think she didn't mean it after all? That he was so irresistible that now even after all the hurtful words he had flung at her she would swallow her pride and stay? If he had made just one move, said just one encouraging word, she would have done exactly that. But he didn't.

'Goodbye, Elliott,' she said in a voice that sounded cracked and raw. Then somehow she found the strength to walk out of his life and not look behind her as she did so.

Her mother had been delighted to see Cassie back.

While not actually saying 'I told you so', she expressed little surprise and a good deal of pleasure at her daughter's sudden appearance on the doorstep of the house the Russells owned in one of London's more exclusive squares. She offered her sobbing daughter consolation and comfort, but never suggested that a reconciliation might take place.

'So you've left him. I wondered how long it would be,' she said with a barely concealed satisfaction. 'Your father and I knew no good would come of it, but you would insist on marrying him. You could have done so much better for yourself. It's not too late, Cassie. You still can.'

'I loved him,' Cassie protested, aware even as she spoke the words that they were in the past tense. Was it really over, then? She could hardly believe that Elliott, the man whose forceful personality had, a few short months ago, swept her completely off her feet, would let her go easily.

'But did he love you, my dear, or were you just a passing fancy?' her mother asked acidly, planting a seed of doubt in Cassie's mind for the first time. 'Oh, he thought enough of you to marry you, I know, but with a girl with your background he could hardly do otherwise——' Mrs Russell's well-bred features expressed misgivings.

'It's not over. It can't be,' Cassie protested.

But, as the days passed and Elliott did not appear at the house or make any attempt to contact her as she had confidently expected, it seemed as if her mother was right. Perhaps he did not care any more. Perhaps he had already done as he had threatened and had found a substitute for his errant wife. Numbly Cassie digested the fact that Elliott was not going to make the first move. If she wanted him back it was up to her to do something about it. She must go and talk to him, ex-

plain that she had spoken hastily—that they both had
—and suggest that they tried again.

'I think you're making a great mistake, my dear,'
Mrs Russell commented when Cassie confided her plan
of going along to the flat, ostensibly to collect her
clothes, in fact to try to reason her way back to her
husband's affections. 'But go if you must.'

And so she picked a time in the early evening when
she thought Elliott was sure to be home and, dressed in
an outfit that she knew he particularly liked, with her
hair done in an attractive style, she set out for the flat.
Her heart pounded as she walked up the stairs to the
second floor, spurning the commissionaire's offer of the
lift in the hope that the walk would steady her frayed
nerves. She paused for a second or two outside the
familiar door, then took a deep breath and rang the
bell, wishing desperately that the words would come to
her to heal the breach between them when Elliott appeared. But when the door was wrenched impatiently
open and he stood before her, darkly attractive as ever
in a casual sweater and well-fitting slacks that accentuated his powerful frame, she hesitated before breaking
into speech.

'Cassandra!' His expression was thunderstruck.

'Yes. I——'

'I thought you weren't coming back.'

Hardly the most welcoming of words, but after all,
she had caught him off balance. She braced herself and
said steadily, 'I had to see you. Elliott, can't we try
again? I'm sure that if we both tried, if we both wanted
to make it work, there would be a chance.'

What his answer might have been, she did not know.
She even fooled herself into thinking that there was a
warmth in his eyes which heralded a reconciliation
between them. But, as she took a step towards him, a

strange voice sounded from somewhere behind him in the flat.

'Elliott, love, I can't find——' The words broke off suddenly as the owner of the voice, a small attractive blonde, apparently clad only in a brief towelling bathrobe, appeared in the hall and realised that Elliott had the front door open. 'Oops, sorry!' She vanished in the direction of the bedroom, clutching the robe to her.

'Liz!' Elliott started after her, then turned back to Cassie.

'I see you didn't waste too much time in looking for a replacement for me,' she said bitterly.

'Look, Cassandra, it's not what you're thinking——'

'Isn't it?' she asked. 'Come on, Elliott, I wasn't born yesterday. I suppose you gave me fair warning that this might happen. I'm just surprised that you've found someone else so quickly. Foolish of me really, isn't it? I'd forgotten how successful you always were with the ladies.'

'If only you could see——'

'I think I've seen all I want to see,' she said coldly, and then, feeling suddenly sick at the scene she had just witnessed, she turned and ran from the door as if all the fiends of hell were after her. She thought she heard him call out after her, but she did not stop her headlong flight. She wasn't prepared to hear whatever lame excuses he had to offer. Outside in the road she saw a taxi for hire and hailed it, giving her parents' address in a voice that shook with reaction.

At home, in the luxurious bedroom which had been hers since she was a child, she cried her heart out at Elliott's betrayal. It was there that her mother found her some hours later, lying in the dark in a crumpled, tear-stained heap on top of the bed.

'He's not worth it, Cassie,' Mrs Russell told her

firmly, as, in between helping to bathe her daughter's ravaged face, she extracted the story of the visit to the flat. 'In future, I hope you'll be guided by me and your father. Believe me, we know what's best for you. You're only twenty. You've your whole life before you and you'll soon forget Elliott Grant.'

And Cassie, hardly caring enough to put up a fight against the process, had allowed herself to slip back into the secure, protected cocoon of her childhood again. For a while she hoped against hope that Elliott might care enough to offer some explanation for his behaviour, but she received no word from him. When, one day, the rest of her belongings were delivered by taxi with not even a covering letter from him, she knew that it was time to try and put him and her brief period of married life behind her.

She fell in with her mother's wishes, going with her on an extended tour of the Continent that Mrs Russell had wanted to take for years, but had never managed to prise her husband away from his business interests for long enough to achieve it. She was entirely happy to accept her daughter as a substitute and if, occasionally, she noticed Cassie's smile was a little forced or her attention inclined to wander, she was wise enough not to comment on the fact.

After six months away from England Cassie returned with glowing good health, a set of smart new clothes and the knowledge that, far from forgetting Elliott, he still haunted her dreams as well as her waking hours. How could she take an interest in any of the young, eligible men whom her mother invited to parties for her benefit when she was constantly comparing them with the man who was, after all, still her husband? How could she concentrate on enjoying herself as her mother recommended when wherever she went in London she was searching for a glimpse of his tall figure in the crowded streets?

There would be a divorce some time, she supposed drearily. She imagined that she could petition for her freedom on the grounds of Elliott's adultery with the unknown woman, but she shrank from the messiness of it all as well as the possible necessity for her to confront him in court. She was hardly going to want to leap headlong into matrimony with someone else, however eligible and good-looking, so soon after her present disillusion. At the moment Cassie hardly cared if she never went out with a man, attractive or otherwise, again, but she supposed the pain would pass. Far better to let the years pass and then quietly to submit evidence to the courts that she and Elliott had lived apart and lost contact and therefore that the marriage had broken down irretrievably. After all, that was only the simple truth.

In the meantime the only sure solution was to get away and find a job of some sort abroad. Perhaps demanding work in a new environment would help her to forget her disastrous marriage and recover from the misery it had brought her. Cassie anticipated a struggle with her mother over the question, but, surprisingly, Mrs Russell had put no obstacles in her way and had even used her contacts to secure Cassie an interview with a London property firm which specialised in selling holiday homes in various parts of Europe.

'They've got other applicants for this job in France, of course,' she told Cassie, 'but Serena Davenport assured me that you would have it unless you came over at interview as totally incompetent. She went so far as to promise me that.'

'But that's hardly fair,' Cassie protested. 'What about the other people applying?'

'They'd do exactly the same in your shoes,' Mrs Russell said firmly. 'And really, my dear, if you're absolutely set on getting a job, you may as well take this chance. It's not as if you're going to find much else without qualifications.'

That was true enough, Cassie reflected soberly. An education at a 'superior' school where the emphasis had been more upon turning out young ladies than on ensuring the pupils secured the requisite number of exam results to find a good job or place at university, followed by two years at a Swiss finishing school, had given her poise and polish, but very little else of practical value when it came to earning a living. But then there had been no need to think about such things before now. Elliott had been right when he had told her she was spoilt, she thought to herself.

She sailed through the interview with a breezy confidence that she was far from feeling and was genuinely relieved to find that her moderate typing skills along with her one asset, the fluent French she had acquired in Switzerland, carried far greater weight than the fact that she was her mother's daughter. After a brief training period in the London office she was to be sent out to Provence for the summer months with the possibility of remaining there on the permanent staff if she worked hard and showed an aptitude for the business.

That had been over four years ago now and she was still here in Provence, a land that she had grown to love and admire more as time passed by. It was a place of violent contrasts, offering warmth and blinding light at the same time as harshness and poverty. It stretched from the flat marshes of the coastal region where the famed white horses of the Camargue roamed free inland to the small scattered villages perched atop bare hillsides where peasants scratched a living from the land just as their ancestors had toiled centuries before them. It was a land of scorching summer suns and icy mistrals, a place where the Romans had conquered and settled and where now modern tourists flocked in their thousands every year.

And she enjoyed her work. At least, Cassie amended, coming back to the present with a start as Mrs Clarke's sharp voice reminded her that she had nearly overshot the turning which led to their hotel, she found the job challenging and generally got on well with the people she had to ferry around the countryside. Of course there were exceptions and the Clarkes were among them. But so far one of the pluses of the job was the host of friends she had made, many of whom had initially been clients of the firm for whom she worked.

As yet, although the striking combination of her flaming hair, pale skin and undeniably feminine figure attracted many men to her, none had even managed to stir her senses the way that Elliott had done without even trying. But at least she now no longer kept to the nun-like seclusion in which she had lived when she had first come out to France. Now she accepted invitations and had built up a reasonably active social life. The insecure girl who had picked her way out of the ruins of her marriage and had determined to stand on her own feet in future had grown up and learned how to cope with anything that life cared to throw at her.

CHAPTER TWO

AND surely, thought Cassie, her mouth twitching with sudden humour, life couldn't produce any greater terrors than the Clarkes. She parked the car in front of their plush four-star hotel, helped them out of their seats, and bade them a restrained farewell, hoping fervently that she never saw them again. The couple mellowed sufficiently to thank her in grudging fashion for her trouble and threatened to pay another visit to the office in the morning.

'Please do. We'll be happy to help you,' she smiled, thanking her stars that it was her turn to stay on in the office and attend to the paperwork the following day. 'My colleague, Monsieur Pinot, will be delighted to show you some of the other properties on our books.'

'Well, at least it'll make a change having a man to show us round,' Mrs Clarke said briskly, pleased with the idea.

'Even if he is a foreigner,' her husband added doubtfully.

And on that note they went inside the hotel, leaving Cassie free to give vent to the laughter which she had struggled successfully to hide in their presence. Poor Jules, she thought, as she drove away. He was going to have problems if the Clarkes did decide to continue house-hunting tomorrow.

She was still smiling as she parked the car and walked through one of the narrow streets of the old town, past the cathedral of St Trophime, to the tree-lined square where McIlroy and Wentworth had their offices. After the blinding sunshine outside the cool dimness of the outer office where she worked was a blessed relief and Cassie slumped into her chair and kicked off her shoes with an air of abandon.

'So you're back at last.' Jules, the senior assistant by virtue of the fact that he had been employed six months longer than she had, swung round from his untidy, paper-strewn desk at the other side of the room and prepared to talk.

'Did you think I'd got lost again? Come on, Jules, I'm a good girl now.' It was a standing joke between them that when Cassie had first taken clients out on her own she had regularly got herself and her passengers lost in the depths of the sun-baked countryside and Jules had lost count of the number of times he had been sent in search of her. She smiled affectionately at him now. Only two years older than herself, Jules Pinot was a pleasant enough workmate with his ready, if occasionally slightly malicious, sense of humour and the keen intelligence that Cassie often envied when she got into difficulty with paperwork and was forced to ask his assistance. Not that he wasn't all too eager to help her in the office and he had hinted more than once that their easy working relationship could be extended outside business hours if she cared to try the experiment. Cassie had never taken him up on the offer, reluctant to mix her office life with her social activities, and he had accepted her decision without rancour, probably, she suspected, because he rarely lacked for female company when he wanted it; he had a smooth charm that would appeal to most women.

'You're late back,' he said, glancing at the clock.

'I was having problems with the English couple I took round. They're coming in tomorrow and I don't envy you having to tote them round.' She launched into a description of the day's activities, expecting him to share her amusement. Then, realising from his lack of response that he wasn't really interested in what she was saying, she stopped and asked, 'Jules, has something happened?'

'You could say that.' He studied her for a moment, his brown eyes dancing tantalisingly. 'I wonder if you'll have a better effect on him than I did. He looks the type who'd respond to a little feminine charm.'

'Who does?' Cassie demanded, completely bewildered. 'What are you talking about?'

'The boss man from head office who arrived this afternoon.' Jules shrugged. 'I suppose we should have suspected something of the sort after that take-over by Prospect Properties a couple of months back. You remember all the fuss there was over that.'

'Yes.' She had a vivid memory of the anxious days they had gone through. Mr Thompson, their easy-going boss, had thirty years' experience in the property world, but he had feared for his job, scared that he would be given a golden handshake and his post offered to a younger man. For all his casual air and confident assertions that he could find work anywhere, Jules had been worried too. And Cassie herself, with less to lose than the other two, had been distinctly nervous nevertheless. She had wondered if her new-found freedom would disappear with her employment and she would find herself crawling back to London with her tail between her legs, dependent once more on her parents. But nothing so drastic had taken place. 'All that happened was that a directive was sent round to all branches telling us to carry on as usual. We didn't hear any more about the take-over. So what's wrong now?'

'Who knows?' Jules gave a expressive wave of his hands and lapsed into the French that Cassie now had few problems in understanding. 'He arrived out of the blue, strode in as if he owned the place and talked to me as if I was the office boy. He was pretty annoyed not to find Monsieur Thompson here at his desk.'

Cassie pulled a sympathetic face. After the time she had spent working with him she was well acquainted with Mr Thompson's habits and his long lunch breaks were one of his little indulgences. Often they stretched, Provençal fashion, until the late afternoon. 'What happened?'

'Oh, I made excuses, which he patently didn't believe. I said Monsieur Thompson was out with a client, I thought. That he would not be long. And then we sat either side of the desk watching the minutes ticking by.' The young Frenchman winced at the memory of what had obviously been an uncomfortable episode. 'When he turned up at half-past three stinking of *vin du pays* and garlic, he wasn't very popular, to put it mildly.'

'So?' she queried.

'So they've been closeted together ever since then and I imagine he's getting the same sort of dressing-down I got for having my feet up on the desk when he came in. It's stupid to expect us to work London hours down here in the South of France, but he didn't seem to think so.'

'You mean he's still here?'

'Ssh! Keep your voice down,' Jules warned her quickly as she spoke louder than usual out of sheer surprise.

'But it's nearly five. What can he have been saying to Mr Thompson all that time?'

'Well, he can't be giving him the sack, if that's what you're thinking. From the look of him I hardly think he'd waste that much of his valuable time dismissing someone.'

Cassie licked suddenly dry lips apprehensively. 'Did he ask to see me?'

'Demand is a better description. I told him where you were. I expect the summons will come when he's finished wiping the floor with our revered boss,' Jules said casually. 'Unless, of course, you'd like to go and announce your return to the office?'

'No, thanks,' she said hastily. 'From the sound of him so far I think I can delay the pleasure of meeting this ogre from head office. What's he like? Old or young?'

'Planning your strategy accordingly?' Her colleague raised a quizzical brow.

She grinned. 'There's nothing like knowing the enemy before you meet him. Well?'

'He's no old man whose crusty exterior hides a heart of pure gold, if that's what you're hoping for. In his thirties, I'd say, and he acts like a lord of creation. As you'll have gathered, I didn't take to him. But you——' He broke off and gave her a calculating glance.

'But I——?' she prompted him.

'You may feel differently about him.'

'Why?'

Jules shrugged. 'I shouldn't think there's a female heart with a thirty-mile radius that's immune to him. I imagine he has quite a way with women when he bothers enough to try his luck.'

'That's a fair compliment,' she said dryly. 'You're not exactly slow off the mark yourself where women are concerned.'

'With notable exceptions,' he countered.

'Rubbish. I refuse to take you seriously and you should be glad of it. Now, tell me more. Is he good-looking?' Cassie was intrigued in spite of herself.

'He's a type women go for,' Jules acknowledged grudgingly. 'And he probably spends a fair amount of time exploiting the fact. But Elliott Grant's no fool for all that, Cassie. Don't think he's just a sucker for a pretty face.'

She felt a cold tremor go down her spine at his words and the smile stiffened on her face. She must have misheard him. It couldn't be. 'Who did you say?'

'Elliott Grant.'

Dear heaven, no! She hadn't made a mistake. For an instant Cassie hoped wildly that it might be someone else who shared the same name, then discounted the idea as quickly. The description Jules had given her fitted Elliott too perfectly. He acted like a lord of creation, Jules had said. Could that be any other than *her* Elliott whose arrogant assumption that he was somehow head and shoulders above other mortals had exasperated her as often as she had reluctantly acknowledged its truth—for her at least. How like him to arrive without any warning and turn everything upside down! He had never been a man who suffered fools gladly, and he tended to rank everyone with whom he did not see eye to eye in that category.

Five years apart. Five years in which she thought that she had learned to cope with everything and everyone. Yet the very idea of meeting Elliott again sent the world spinning around her. She could feel the blood draining from her cheeks and a rushing sound in her ears and she fought desperately to stop herself fainting for the first time in her life. She could not afford to meet him like a half-conscious wreck. She must have all her wits about her for the inevitable confrontation. She was a cool, poised woman now, not a naïve girl. Why couldn't she stop shaking?

'Cassie, are you all right?' From a long way away she heard Jules' anxious voice. 'What's the matter?' He crossed the room to her side and bent over her. 'Are you ill? Can I get you a glass of cognac?'

The universal remedy, thought Cassie, with a weak smile. It was hardly likely to make a good impression if another member of the staff, albeit his errant wife, was wheeled in for interview smelling the worse for drink. 'I'll be fine in a minute, Jules, really,' she assured him feebly, trying to convince herself of the fact at the same time. If she felt like this at the very mention of her husband's presence in the next room, how on earth would she react when they were face to face? 'It must have been the sun. It was very hot today and the Clarkes would pick the middle of the day to start the trip.'

'How many times have I told you to take a hat, *chérie*?' Jules was concerned for her. 'With that pale skin of yours you're asking for trouble going bareheaded. But you are always so stubborn, so English, and you refuse. What am I to do with you, eh?' He perched on the desk beside her and took her hand in his sympathetically, raising his other hand to brush away the heavy swathes of hair away from her face. 'Shall I——'

Cassie never discovered what he was going to suggest. Neither of them had noticed the door of the inner office swinging open and two figures emerging, until the sound of Mr Thompson's shocked voice made them aware that they were no longer alone.

'Miss Russell! Monsieur Pinot! Have you taken leave of your senses?'

Cassie caught her breath and thrust herself away from Jules as if his touch was suddenly red-hot, her cheeks now as flushed as before they had been pale.

'So this is the elusive Miss Russell.' Any hope that this was all a case of mistaken identity was instantly dispelled at the sound of the cool, faintly detached, masculine voice that broke the shocked silence. Damn Elliott for deciding to leave the office at that precise moment and starting their encounter points ahead!

With an effort she raised her head defiantly and looked across at him, standing in the doorway behind Mr Thompson, his tall, powerful figure dwarfing the older man. He hadn't changed much, she thought, as her swift glance took in the familiar, sharply defined features wearing the same look of disenchanted cynicism that she had grown used to watching in that last, bitter period of their life together. His dark eyes flickered with some emotion she could not identify as they met hers, but in that brief instant she sensed that he was not surprised to see her here and wondered why that should be. Trust Elliott to make sure that while the whole world was rocked off balance, he remained cool, calm and totally in control of the situation. But had he known before that she would be here?

'Miss Russell, this is Mr Grant from our head office in London.' Mr Thompson, normally casual in his dealings with his staff, sounded stiffly reproving as he effected the introduction. She guessed that he had not enjoyed his time with Elliott, and the sudden sight of his two office juniors apparently caught exchanging sweet nothings in office hours was not guaranteed to help matters for him.

Beside her Cassie was aware of Jules recovering and heard him offering some attempt at an explanation of their behaviour.

'It's not what you're thinking. We were just——'

Elliott cut him short. 'I have eyes, Monsieur Pinot. I saw what you were doing and I'm more than capable of putting my own construction on it.' His tone made it clear that he was not in the mood to accept excuses. 'I told you earlier about wasting time in the office. I suggest that if you don't want to start looking for work elsewhere you stop playing around and get busy.'

Rashly Cassie sprang to Jules' defence. 'He was only trying to be helpful!'

Her husband's cold gaze rested dispassionately on her flushed face. 'In future he can leave his knight-errantry for outside office hours. And you will be a little less ready to—take advantage—of his good nature from now on,' he said, making it quite clear which of them he felt was really to blame for the episode he had just witnessed. 'In the meantime I'd like to talk to you about your job, if you feel you can spare me the time.'

She opened her mouth to make a tart rejoinder, then realised the rashness of engaging Elliott in a slanging match in front of an interested audience. 'Certainly,' she said coolly, and was aware that she had jolted him. The younger Cassie would have acted more impulsively.

She got hastily to her feet, mentally cursing the recklessness with which she had tossed off her shoes as she scrabbled furiously beneath her desk in an effort to retrieve them. When she had finally found them and put them on she saw that he was holding open the door of the inner office for her to precede him. His air of exaggerated patience did nothing for her composure.

Behind her she heard Mr Thompson attempting to join them and Elliott's decisive voice vetoing the idea. Then the sound of the door closing firmly that indicated that they were alone together. She walked over to the window, staring unseeingly at the bright flowers in the small courtyard outside as she tried desperately to calm her churning emotions. If only she could have had time to get over the first shock of meeting Elliott again! Time to assume a cool exterior, a shell that would withstand the force of his personality and help her to cope with him. But she had been plunged straight into this and he was making full use of the advantage it gave him over her.

She took a deep breath to calm herself, then forced herself to turn and face him. No, Elliott hadn't changed. Five years ago he had been unmistakably an up-and-coming executive, definitely on his way, but not yet at the top. Now there was no doubt that he had made it all the way; less from the trappings of success: the slim gold watch on his wrist; the elegantly tailored suit that fitted his broad shoulders superbly and moulded every line of his tall, athletic form; the snowy white linen, which, despite the heat of the day, retained its crisp perfection; and the gleaming, hand-tooled shoes which held no speck of pavement dust; than from the air of confident authority that clung to him.

He would be in his mid-thirties now, Cassie reminded herself as she studied him, but, for all that, he had kept himself well. There was no trace of surplus flesh on that well-muscled frame to indicate an excess of business lunches. There was no trace of grey as yet in the mane of dark hair that he wore brushed severely back from his forehead and he was tanned and fit. He looked exactly what he was: a man in the peak of condition who knew just what he wanted out of life and anticipated no particular difficulty in obtaining it. And she had the feeling he did not bother overmuch about anyone unfortunate enough to get in his way.

She shivered slightly. She had always been aware that Elliott had a ruthless streak, but until now she had never faced it head-on. When he had courted her the sheer force of his personality and physical appeal had overwhelmed her completely. Now he might find that his child-bride had altered in more ways than one. She might even have the power to surprise him; she had a feeling that she already had.

'Well, Elliott, how are you?' she asked coolly when he made no attempt to break the silence. She was proud of the way she managed to get the words out, sounding careless, casual, as if her entire world had not just been shaken to the foundations by his appearance in front of her like some demon king in a children's pantomime.

He shrugged. 'Five years older. But otherwise much the same.' His dark eyes raked over her enigmatically and she wondered if he was comparing her with the Cassie he had known and was finding her changed for the worse. Perversely, womanlike, she hoped that he was not. If only she had had time to make running repairs to her appearance—at least tidy her hair— instead of confronting him, sunstreaked and unkempt, after a hard day's work.

'And what, exactly, are you doing here?' She put the query as lightly as she could, but it still sounded more like an accusation.

He chose to ignore the question, telling her instead, 'You haven't changed, Cassandra.'

'Did you expect me to?'

'Perhaps. I thought you might have grown up a little,' he said cuttingly. 'But it seems you still put your own pleasures before anything else.'

The nervous tension which had gripped her was fading and in its place she could feel the familiar stirrings of temper. 'Meaning?' she enquired softly.

'You're a very attractive woman and you like men to be aware of it. And when they are you take advantage of them.'

She gave a short laugh. 'Once seen, never forgotten— that's what they always say about me.'

'Do they?' His eyes narrowed. 'You sound as if you lead a pretty hectic social life.'

'So-so.' She was carefully non-committal. It had never paid to reveal all one's cards to Elliott.

'And that young layabout?' He jerked his head contemptuously in the direction of the outer office. 'Where does he come into the scheme of things?'

'Jules?'

'I think that's his name.'

'I don't think that's any of your business,' she told him sharply. 'My private life's my own now. It doesn't concern you any longer, thank God.'

He gave a thin smile. 'Unfortunately for you, I'm afraid that's not the case. It's very much my concern if you intend to devote your office hours to your—affairs.'

He stressed the last word slightly, making it sound deliberately insulting and she flared up instantly. 'I'm not having an affair with Jules!'

'No?' He sounded disbelieving. 'So the tender little scene that I just witnessed meant nothing to you?'

'Nothing at all.'

'From where I was standing I'd say it meant quite a lot to him. Does the poor sucker know that you couldn't care less about him? That he's only around to amuse you in the office when you get bored? How many others do you have waiting for you at home?'

'You know nothing at all about it,' she blazed at him. 'I've worked darned hard since I've been at this office. I don't think you'll find that Mr Thompson has any complaints about me.'

'On the contrary, he gave head office glowing reports of your work here. But how much truth there is in what he said, I've yet to discover. Knowing what I do of you I should imagine his high praises are hardly worth the paper they're written on.'

'You don't know me any more, Elliott. Five years is a long time,' Cassie reminded him.

'You haven't altered. You still think the world should revolve around you, don't you? Well, you may have been able to charm Thompson into turning a blind eye to your activities, but I think you'll find I'm a tougher nut to crack. I'm impervious to your wiles. You're my wife, remember.'

'I was your wife,' she corrected firmly.

'Not in the eyes of the law.'

She shrugged. 'Neither of us has wanted to remarry so far. But a divorce on the grounds of our separation will only be a formality when one of us needs our freedom. Don't worry, Elliott, nothing would induce me to ever live with you again.'

'I don't remember asking you to,' he said coldly. 'After the fiasco that was your idea of marriage I think I could have survived quite happily without setting eyes on you for the rest of my life.'

'If you feel so strongly about it, I'm surprised you didn't do just that,' she said, hitting back, although she felt strangely hurt at the bitter note in his voice.

'Where business is concerned personal feelings take second place,' he told her dismissively.

'Of course. How could I have forgotten your devotion to duty?' she asked him. 'Tell me, Elliott, are you happy giving all your time to the world of high finance? Does your success in wheeling and dealing compensate for your failure in other fields?'

She was playing with fire and she knew it. Elliott's temper had always been uncertain at the best of times and although he was five years older now she somehow doubted if he was any more capable of holding on to his control. And her barb had gone home; of that she was sure. As she faced the powerful figure blocking her only line of escape she wondered if she had been a little too eager to bait him.

But he surprised her. Apparently unmoved by her taunt, he merely looked cynically amused. 'What makes you think I'm a failure in any field?' he queried with all his old arrogance.

'Does being King Rat in the City rat-pack really compensate for coming home to a cold house and an empty bed?'

'I'm sorry if I'm shattering any of your girlish illusions, Cassandra, but what makes you think it has to compensate for either?'

She floundered, suddenly aware of the naïvety of her statement. She, of all people, should know only too well that Elliott was not a man to deprive himself of female companionship just because the woman he had married was away from the scene. Firmly she blanked her mind to the memories of an attractive blonde who called Elliott her love with such a proprietorial air. 'You haven't approached me about a divorce,' she pointed out.

'I haven't needed to. My dear Cassandra, I'd have thought that even you would have realised that a man doesn't offer marriage to every woman he goes to bed with.'

'Don't patronise me!'

'I thought I was enlightening your naïve little mind. But then I was forgetting, you're not exactly ignorant of such matters yourself, are you?'

Tempted to an angry denial, she thought better of it and smiled sweetly at him instead. 'You could hardly expect me to be, living in a country where every man I meet is more than willing to help further my romantic education.'

He gave a harsh laugh. 'I wouldn't have thought romance came into it very much.' He took a step towards her, studying her with insulting deliberation. 'Or are soft lights and sweet music a necessary part of the seduction scene to quell any pangs of conscience you might be expected to feel about the husband you left behind you?'

'Hardly,' she lied. 'After all this time apart it would have been an effort to call your face to mind.'

'Or those of the countless other men who've graced your bed since you left me, I imagine.'

Without conscious thought her hand rose from her side and made hard contact with his face. 'How dare you?' she breathed furiously.

He moved forward and, although she stood her ground, she quailed inwardly before the blaze of anger in his eyes. 'How dare I?' he repeated softly. 'Quite easily, Cassandra, believe me. You should learn that when you provoke a man he tends to retaliate in kind.'

'If you hit me, I'll scream the place down,' she warned him, backing away.

His arms reached out for her, fastening round her like steel bands and forcing her to move closer to him instead. 'I was taught never to strike a lady,' he said grimly, stilling her struggles to escape with frightening ease. 'And, although I'm not entirely sure whether you merit the description, I'll give you the benefit of the doubt. But this is what'll happen instead if you try that sort of trick again.'

His head bent towards hers and, knowing only too well what his next action would be, she redoubled her efforts to be free of him, twisting and writhing impotently in his arms. Then his lips came down on hers with a mastery that she could not evade. It was a bruising, hurtful kiss from a man she would have been wiser not to have driven to this pitch of anger. There was none of the remembered tenderness that he had used with her all that time ago when he had gently broken down her inhibitions and had taught her what it meant to abandon herself totally to the pleasures of physical fulfilment. Then his gentleness had masked his hard impatience to make her his as he had matched his eagerness to her untutored immaturity. But then she had been an all too willing participant.

Now she fought him, trying vainly to break free from the insistent pressure of his mouth as he forced her lips apart and began a brutal assault on her senses. Desperately she withheld a response to his practised lovemaking, ignoring the familiar waves of sensation that ran through her at his touch. It had been five years since her whole body had come alive at a man's closeness to her. And now he was taking her in hate and anger, not love, and her traitorous senses still flamed at his nearness.

He pressed her closer to him, moulding her body to every line of his. Now she was fighting herself as well as him, determined not to succumb to an inner voice that was urging her to stop resisting, to give herself up to the mindless ecstasy that his kisses offered her, to forget that this was the man who five years ago had betrayed her and who five minutes ago had been accusing her of the worst sins he could throw at her. Elliott had made it exceedingly clear what he thought of her and if she gave in now he would despise her even more. Yet how long could she hold out against such an insidious attack?

But then it was over. Even as she relaxed, subdued and quiescent in his arms, preparing to betray herself and surrender totally to him, he released her suddenly and stepped away as if the sight of her disgusted him. He was breathing hard, but, unlike her, seemed completely in control of himself. As she reeled back he held out a chair by the desk for her and said abruptly, 'You'd better sit down before you fall down.'

Cassie allowed him to push her towards the seat and sank into it weakly. 'It's all right. I'm not going to faint.' She spoke to herself as much as to him.

'I'm relieved to hear it.' He didn't sound over-concerned. She supposed he would have coped with all his usual competence if she had crumpled to the floor. Nothing ever threw Elliott, she recalled. 'Does one kiss normally have such an effect on you?'

'Can't you remember?' she asked acidly. 'Or have you made love to so many women since I left you that you find it hard to tell them apart?'

'Be careful! I've given you fair warning, Cassandra. You've only yourself to blame if you distract me again.'

Distract him! Was that what he called it? She hardly knew whether she was on her head or her heels, but one thing was certain in her mind after this little episode.

She and Elliott had nothing in common any more and the sooner they applied for a divorce the better as far as she was concerned.

She pressed her hand to her mouth which still ached from the force of his kiss and tried to collect herself. She looked across the room at him and quickly glanced away when she found him gazing directly at her, a frown creasing his forehead.

'You didn't always find my kisses so offensive,' he observed.

If only he knew how close she had been to demonstrating that, whatever she thought of the man himself, his lovemaking still had the power to stir her. Thank God, he hadn't realised. 'I seem to remember that I used to have some choice in the matter,' she retorted.

He sighed impatiently and ran a hand through his hair, disturbing its severe neatness. 'For God's sake, pull yourself together and stop acting as if I'd tried to rape you. Isn't it a little late in the day for outraged modesty on your part?'

'I didn't realise that the *droit du seigneur* still operated and that submitting to the embraces of the men from head office was part of my duties out here. Forgive me for not being a little more willing. I suppose I should thank you for the honour you've done me,' she said sarcastically.

'It won't happen again—if you behave yourself.' He strode over to the desk and sat down facing her across its untidy surface. 'We've spent enough time exchanging pleasantries. Perhaps we can get down to business now.'

'We could have done so a lot earlier as far as I was concerned.'

'Then you've only yourself to blame for taking me off on other tacks.' He looked straight at her and held her reluctant gaze. 'Do you think it's possible that we could behave like the two sensible adults we're supposed to be for the next few minutes? I've a fair amount to cover and I've wasted enough time already.'

'Go ahead,' she said rudely. 'I'm all ears.'

He ignored the comment and continued, 'Cassandra, whether you like it or not, I'm here for the next two months to see how the business can be improved and stepped up at this end. When I learnt that you were working here I thought that there might be a little awkwardness between us initially, but I hoped that you would have sense enough by now to treat the matter calmly, as I intend to do.'

'Your behaviour just now being a sample of that, I suppose?' she asked him.

'If you choose to kick up a fuss, I've given you a sample of what to expect. If you accept the situation, I'll treat you like an adult instead of like a spoiled brat. Which is it to be?'

'I don't have a great deal of option, do I?' she replied, and went on hastily, seeing the impatience in his face, 'All right, I'm perfectly prepared to be civilised about it all. In fact, I'll be more than happy to forget that there was ever anything between us. I reverted to my maiden name when I started work for McIlroy and Wentworth, so there are no problems there. As far as I'm concerned I've never met you before. Does that satisfy you?'

'Perfectly.' His voice was clipped and completely devoid of emotion.

'I'd hate your bosses at head office to be accusing you of favouring the office junior because you happened to be married to her,' she taunted him. 'It might stand in the way of your promotion chances.'

He looked amused. 'I hardly think so.'

'They have such a high opinion of you?' she enquired sceptically.

'The people at head office do what I tell them to do. Their ideas about me, flattering or unflattering, don't interest me very much.'

'You were always an arrogant bastard, Elliott. Do you have to act as if you own the whole show?'

'With justification, this time.'

'You mean——' The implication suddenly dawned on her.

'I mean that I am Prospect Properties,' he told her with some satisfaction.

She sat in stunned silence for a moment, then, recovering her poise, said, 'Congratulations. You must have worked hard.'

'I usually get what I want.'

Except when it came to personal relationships, she qualified silently. But perhaps, even there, Elliott pleased himself. With the girl he had never really wanted to marry safely out of his life, the way was open for him to dally with any woman of his choice without being trapped into offering marriage to any of them. 'I suppose you do,' she acknowledged. 'I'm only surprised that now you're the big boss you've time to worry about one small corner of the empire.'

'I have an eye for small details,' he said. 'As you'll realise when I start getting to grips with the work in the office here. I expect to look into every aspect of the day-to-day running of the business.'

'I hope you find it a profitable exercise.'

'Oh, I expect to.' He got to his feet and instinctively she rose too, feeling overpowered by the tall frame looming over her. 'I think that's all for now. Any questions?'

So far as he was concerned she might have been any employee receiving instructions from a new boss. Well, if he could assume that attitude and make it convincing, so could she. 'Not at the moment, thank you,' she said coolly, and turned to go. Her hand was on the door when he called her back.

'Cassandra——'

She paused. 'Yes?'

'Don't presume upon your past relationship with me. That's dead and buried. I won't help you out of any trouble you find yourself in. I expect hard work from my staff and I don't make allowances—for anyone.'

'Don't worry,' she assured him crisply. 'Taking advantage of you is the last thing on my mind.' Then, without looking to see how he had received her parting shot, she opened the door and headed for the sanity of the outer office.

CHAPTER THREE

IT was long after office hours and Mr Thompson had disappeared, probably eager to go home and recover from the day's unpleasant experiences. But Jules was waiting for her, a faintly anxious expression on his face.

'Cassie? You're all right? I was beginning to wonder what he was up to in there with you.'

She gave a short laugh. 'There was no need, I can assure you. Seduction was never further from a man's thoughts, although I think murder entered his head a couple of times.'

'I thought you might have taken a fancy to him.'

'Hardly. I've rarely come across anyone I've disliked so much.' Cassie picked up her bag and crossed to the door. 'Come on, let's get out of here before he changes his mind about letting me escape from his clutches.'

'I'll see you home,' Jules offered, obviously wanting to talk, and for once Cassie did not discourage him. After the shock of seeing Elliott again she was in the mood to appreciate kindness from any source and was past bothering whether it might lead to future complications.

They left the office and set off together across the square and back into the old quarter of the town. Jules had scoffed at her when she had turned down the chance of her own flat some distance from the office, dismissing her preference for lodgings with kindly Madame Martin in one of the old red-tiled houses near the cathedral as 'sentimental rubbish'.

She had laughed and argued the question, although she had no intention of letting him change her mind.

She had had enough of other people trying to organise her life. It was time she struck out on her own and held out for her own ideas. 'It's the atmosphere that gets to me. Do you realise that there were people living in the same area over two thousand years ago? Probably ordinary people going out to work for a living just like you or me.'

Jules snorted. 'I'm surprised that you don't go the whole hog and find a mud hut to live in as they probably did.'

'That shows how little you know about it,' she retorted. 'The Romans were responsible for some marvellous buildings here. Look at the theatre that they built when they colonised Arles. They made it big enough to seat twelve thousand people and——'

'Spare me the details, please!' He held up his hands in mock horror. 'All I know is that now it's just another old ruin littering up the place and no earthly use to anyone. It's about time they pulled the rest down and built something modern there.'

'Holiday flats, I suppose. Would you approve of that?'

'Yes, I would. They'd be a darned sight more use to people,' he told her.

'Philistine!' she accused him, and then had laughed and given up trying to convince him of her point of view. It was no use losing one's temper with Jules; he just treated it as a joke and refused to get in the least offended. Which, she reflected, considering her own tendency to flare up on every possible occasion, probably did a lot to contribute to their relatively harmonious office relationship.

Not that things would be particularly happy in the immediate future. Elliott proposed staying for two months and Cassie had a strong feeling that there might be a few storms to be weathered during that period. He certainly didn't seem to have started on a particularly conciliatory note.

Jules echoed her thoughts. 'So you're out of favour with Elliott Grant too?'

'You could say that.'

'And I thought you were sure to charm him. Is the man blind or just a misogynist?'

'Perhaps I have the wrong colour hair for him.' She pulled a rueful face and wondered what her companion would say if she told him that once she had been so far in favour with their new boss that he had promised to love and cherish her until death did them part. Instead she said, 'I think we'll have to tread fairly carefully for the next few weeks.'

'He's got the temper of the devil—that much I did establish,' Jules told her. 'As the Bible says, a soft answer turns away anger. Perhaps we will put it into practice.'

And a fat lot of good it'll do us, Cassie thought dismally as she bade him farewell and let herself into her landlady's spotlessly shining hallway and ascended the stairs to her set of rooms at the top of the house. The wooden shutters were drawn across the windows to keep out the heat of the day and the atmosphere in the little sitting room was cool, dim and pleasantly restful after the vexations of the last few hours. She went into the tiny kitchen which led off it and poured herself a long iced fruit drink from a bottle in the refrigerator, then wandered back to collapse in one of the ancient armchairs with her feet up and think over the situation in which she found herself.

Fate must have decided that everything was going a little too smoothly for Cassandra Russell and determined to throw a bit of misfortune in her direction, she mused sourly. This morning she had set off for work without a care in the world and now she felt as if the heavens had fallen on top of her.

Damn Elliott for having the upper hand, she thought resentfully. She wondered how long it had taken him to come to terms with the prospect of meeting his errant wife again. The fact that even if she had known in advance what to expect she would still have been unable to think of any way of dealing with it was no consolation at all to her. Elliott had certainly not given the impression of a man at a loss as to how to act. On the contrary, she thought, wincing at the memory, he had shown no hesitation in choosing precisely the means necessary to intimidate her and ensure her co-operation.

Not that he had needed to exert much energy to achieve that end. Cassie remembered the way he had stilled her struggles with arrogant ease. He was not to know, of course, that her irrational impulse to give up the fight the moment his mouth had touched hers had contributed more than anything else to his effortless conquest of her. How feeble he must have thought her! Hardly worth the trouble of putting her in her place, really. He had only done it to demonstrate that whatever ideas she might have acquired during their parting about her own ability to survive, she was fated to acknowledge his superiority over her still. And she had done just that.

Her lips firmed decisively. If Elliott thought he could still walk all over her, he had another think coming! He had knocked her off balance and had taken advantage of the situation. But next time she would be well prepared. Rigidly Cassie closed her mind to the stirrings of an inner voice that recognised Elliott's physical magnetism for her and told herself that she was imagining things. How could any woman actually enjoy the kind of rough treatment that he had meted out to her?

For two days she saw little of him and told herself

that she was glad of it. But, on the third day, he came into the outer office for a while to issue authoritative instructions to Jules about some business that had been neglected and she found herself studying him closely, unable to convince herself that the man she had once loved so passionately and whom she had thought returned that feeling could have changed so radically. That devotion was no longer directed towards her. Some other woman would be the recipient of all his charm and his practised caresses. Someone else would glory in the feel of that lithe, hard-muscled body pressing against hers, demanding a response which she would be unable to deny him. And she was welcome to him, whoever she was, thought Cassie, determinedly returning her attention to the pile of papers in front of her and ignoring the way her senses clamoured as he left the other desk and came to stand at her side.

He was near enough for her to catch a whiff of the tangy aftershave he wore, the same sort that Cassie had bought him the first Christmas of their marriage. Did he remember, she wondered, how he had torn off the wrappings and not said a word about the boring predictability of her choice of gift for him until her laughter had got the better of her and she had produced his real present, an original oil painting, commissioned from an artist whose work she knew he admired.

'It was going to be a study of wild life,' she told him with mock humility as he looked it over carefully. 'But when I went to talk to him about it, he decided that there wasn't anything wilder than yours truly and he'd paint me or nothing. I suppose I should be flattered. He doesn't take commissions for portraits usually.'

'I can understand why he made an exception in your case,' Elliott told her.

She asked him anxiously, 'Do you like it?'

'It's superb. He's really caught an exact likeness of

you. And the skin tones are yours to the life. But——'

'But?'

He reached for her and kissed her with lazy thorough-
ness, well aware of the response that flamed within her.
He pushed her back on the bed and joined her there,
shedding his robe as he did so. 'But I prefer the
original,' he said thickly, and those were the last co-
herent words either of them had spoken for some considerable time.

She wondered what had happened to that portrait.
Did it still hang in a place of honour on his office wall
in the City or had it been discreetly removed and
banished to an attic somewhere—or a dustbin? She supposed she was hardly likely to discover its fate. Elliott
was making it very plain that their relationship was
strictly a business one. She would be asking for trouble
if she tried to put things back on any kind of personal
basis. At least she was to be spared the added embarrassment of having the sorry ending of her marriage made
public. To have to deal with Elliott with interested
spectators analysing every move would have been more
than she could have borne.

She crouched over the papers on her desk, pretend-
ing a deep and absorbing fascination with the details of
a holiday home, newly vacant near Saint-Gilles, rather
than look up and acknowledge Elliott's presence. It
was pointless as well as childish, she knew, to try to
ignore that potent blend of masculine attraction by her
side, but she attempted it all the same.

'Busy?' he asked casually.

'Yes, I am rather pressed this morning,' she told him,
not looking up.

A strong brown hand came into her line of vision as,
without apology, he seized upon the house description
and glanced speedily over it. 'You might find that you
have more time on your hands if you didn't find it

necessary to read everything twice. You've spent the last five minutes looking over this.'

He would have noticed that, she thought resentfully. And, what was worse, if he'd taken into his head to ask her what features the house in question possessed, she would have had to confess her total ignorance. 'I didn't realise that you were a time and motion man, Mr Grant,' she said sweetly, giving him a falsely bright smile. 'I can see we're going to have to look to our laurels in future.'

'If you have any.' His tone doubted it. 'Slowness never impresses anyone, least of all our clients. They expect speed and efficiency.'

'Have you ever heard the story of the tortoise and the hare?' she asked him.

He laughed. 'Children's stories are for children, Miss Russell. You may believe in them—I certainly don't. But you'll have a chance to test out your theories to-morrow. I've decided to come out with you for the day and see how you handle the practical side of the business.'

She opened her mouth in instinctive protest, then thought better of it and remained silent. He had every right to accompany her and she had none to refuse him.

Her face must have mirrored her feelings, for a faint glint of amusement showed in his dark eyes. 'There's no need to worry, you know. Your colleague, Monsieur Pinot, survived the experience in more or less one piece. If you're good at your job, there should be no problems.'

'And what happens if you consider that I'm not earning my salary here?'

'It may be necessary to review the situation,' he told her, viewing the matter with apparent calm. 'We may have to find another niche for your undoubted talents, if that's the case.'

'I'm not used to being put on trial, Mr Grant. You may find that you have to make allowances.'

'As I believe I've already told you, I don't make allowances for my staff. But they tell me I have a soft spot where your sex are concerned.'

'Indeed?' she said with deceptive innocence. 'And are "they" right?'

His gaze raked over her with cool indifference, resting slightly longer than necessary at the base of her throat where the open neck of her blouse exposed the expanse of creamy skin and gave a tantalising hint of her firm breasts. Aware of his scrutiny, she fought the urge to do up her top button. *That* would only amuse him.

He took his time about answering and hardly pleased her when he did so. 'That depends on the individual and what she has to offer me,' he said with a derisive smile.

'I may have to disappoint you there.'

'You never know, Miss Russell. I shan't hold it against you so long as you do your best to please.' And on that parting note he went into the other office, leaving Cassie fuming impotently.

'What was all that about?' Jules had been an eager witness to the exchange between them.

'You heard.' Cassie feigned ignorance.

'I heard, but I didn't catch all the undercurrents. I'm eaten up with curiosity as to what it all meant. Has he made a pass at you, *chérie*?'

'Of course not,' she snapped. 'Don't be ridiculous. The man's hardly been here two minutes.'

'It doesn't take long to discover that you are attracted to someone.'

She gave an angry laugh. 'Well, he's got a strange way of showing it, if he is taken with my girlish beauty. Playing cat and mouse with me and making me anxious about my job is no way to win my favours.'

'Strategy,' Jules told her complacently. 'Women always respond to a man who dominates them. He's demonstrating his power.'

'Except he picked the wrong woman if he thought those tactics would impress me,' she said belligerently. 'Anyway, whose side are you, mine or Elliott Grant's?'

He threw up his hands in a gesture of surrender. 'Need you ask? Where you're concerned, *ma belle*, there is no contest. I'm with you all the way. But tell me when war is declared between you and I'll take good care to keep well out of range of the cross-fire.'

'Coward!' she taunted him. 'I thought I might count on you at least to help me stand up to the man.'

'And indeed you can,' he assured her. 'But are you sure that you need any help? You seemed to be giving as good as you got just now.'

'I've certainly no intention of letting him tramp all over me, if that's what you mean.' Cassie tossed her flaming head defiantly. 'He may be an arrogant, domineering, selfish devil, but I can cope with his sort, believe me.'

'Really?' A cool voice sounded immediately behind her and, with a sudden *frisson* of shock she realised that Elliott had re-entered the room. How long had he been standing there and how much had he heard of her confident assertion that she could handle him? In his presence she felt considerably less sure about that statement.

'I——' she gasped. The words that might get her out of the situation refused to come to her mind and she felt like a fish out of water, suddenly desperate for air.

Jules came to her rescue. 'A client,' he clarified the matter smoothly. 'An obnoxious character who's given us all problems at one time or another.'

'Indeed?' There was a sardonic lift to Elliott's brow

as he heard the explanation and for a tense second or two Cassie wondered if he was going to reject it. But it seemed that he thought better of the idea, for he merely turned to her and asked, 'Mr Thompson and I are going through the sales figures for the last six months. Could you find me the file relating to the properties sold in the Arles area, please?'

Silently she got to her feet and went to the opposite side of the room. She found the folder for him and held it out. He took it with a word of thanks and walked back towards the inner office. At the door he turned and said with deceptive gentleness, 'Miss Russell, I'd be obliged if, in future, you kept your opinions of our clients or otherwise to yourself. Not everyone has my forbearing nature and you might find yourself on the receiving end of something unpleasant if anyone decided to retaliate.'

'Do you think that possible?'

'If all your views are delivered with such uncompromising honesty, I'm surprised you've survived this long,' he commented.

'Oh, I'm a survivor all right.'

'I'm relieved to hear it,' he said. 'I'll look forward to seeing you put that philosophy into action tomorrow. It should prove quite an enlightening day in one way or another.'

'I'm glad you think so,' she retorted as he went out and closed the door behind him. In a fit of temper she picked up a book from her desk and hurled it furiously at the wall, wishing that she had had the nerve to throw it at her husband's smoothly controlled features instead.

'I think he won that round,' Jules said appreciatively, laughing at the fury on her face. 'It's no use getting mad at him, Cassie. Like it or not, that's a man who won't crack, however hard you provoke him.'

'No?' She knew him a little better than her colleague did. Well enough to be aware that Elliott could lose his cool with frightening suddenness. And even after five years apart she should have enough sense not to bait him to that pitch. She had already had one demonstration of what was likely to happen if she got across him and she had no desire at all for a repeat performance.

'Take care, *mon enfant*, if you don't want to get your fingers badly burnt. He will fight dirty if you give him half a chance.'

'He won't get the chance, Jules, don't worry about that. Tomorrow I shall be all sweetness and light, the very model of an attentive, hard-working underling, respectful and subservient.'

'If you carry it off for more than five minutes,' he said sceptically, 'I'll give you a reference for the Comédie Française.'

'You'll see,' she told him confidently. 'I always mean what I say. I'll get the upper hand somehow.'

But the next day she felt considerably less assurance as she settled in the driver's seat of the office Citroën and Elliott eased his long limbs into the cramped space by her side. His thigh brushed briefly against hers as he settled himself more comfortably in his seat and she recoiled instinctively at his touch, feeling all the old electricity flare between them at the casual physical contact. It was too much to hope that he hadn't noticed the movement; Elliott had an uncanny knack of noticing everything. But he forbore to comment and she was thankful for it even as she cursed herself for registering his virile attraction.

'You could have driven, you know,' she said abruptly, and then realised how silly the statement sounded. If he'd wanted to take the wheel, he would certainly not have hesitated to tell her so.

He shrugged. 'You're one of the few women I trust in charge of a car,' he told her. 'I've no objection to taking the passenger seat for once.'

Presumably because he had taught her to drive himself, surprising her with the patience he had shown her in the process and giving her both enjoyment and confidence in her growing ability to master the controls.

'I'm glad I can do something right,' she said tartly.

He ignored the comment and continued, 'Besides, I'm only here as an observer today. I want to see exactly how you deal with everything. You sink or swim on your own.'

'I'm quite accustomed to doing that, but thanks for the warning. I suppose that proving that I can handle French roads and French drivers is the first hurdle?'

'If you like,' he said indifferently.

He didn't seem to be in a particularly communicative mood this morning. Cassie glanced at the clear-cut profile beside her and wondered exactly what was biting him today. Was this his normal behaviour with subordinates or could the fact that this particular office junior was his wife be having some bearing on his mood? Even for Elliott, who could handle every awkward problem with the utmost ease, it was a bizarre situation in which to find himself. But he could hardly feel as strange as she did.

'I have to pick up our client, Mr Cox, from his hotel,' she said primly. 'I expect his wife will be joining him. They're looking for a small house to retire to in this area, not too far from civilisation, but with plenty of opportunity for them to get out into the countryside. Mr Cox is keen on wild life and wants to be able to study the creatures on the marshes. His wife, on the other hand, likes town life and wants to be able to see the shops and the bright lights occasionally.'

'And naturally her wishes will take precedence, I

suppose,' he commented cynically.

'We're hoping to hit on somewhere that will suit them both,' Cassie told him sharply, and was unable to resist adding, 'He's a considerate husband. He puts his wife's happiness first.'

'More fool him. I'd have thought he'd have learnt better by now if he's approaching retirement age.'

'Not everyone sees married life the way you do,' she flashed at him.

'There'd be fewer people heading for the divorce courts if they profited by my experience.'

'Really? I'm surprised you consider yourself such an expert with one failed marriage behind you.'

His lips firmed to a thin, uncompromising line. 'It taught me enough to make me think a thousand times before ever contemplating a repeat performance.'

'Be grateful to me for that at least, then,' she said bitterly.

'Oh, I am, Miss Russell, believe me.'

She frowned. 'There's no need to call me that when we're alone together.'

'What would you prefer?' he jeered. 'Mrs Grant? Or perhaps just plain "darling"? Forgive me, I'm not used to the sophisticated world you obviously live in where estranged couples remain the best of friends. Do you want me to forgive and forget and act as if our marriage was a silly boy and girl affair that fizzled out like a damp squib and is best disregarded?'

'You're a fine one to talk about forgiveness!' She threw the words at him, stung by his attitude.

'What do you mean by that?'

'If you don't know, I'm not going to waste time telling you. You've got a remarkably short memory, that's all I can say.'

'Do you blame me for that?' His expression was bleak as he faced her. 'When you've taken an emotional battering, it's sometimes best to try and forget what caused it all.'

'Very convenient. No need to think who might be responsible for it all. What a little plaster saint you are, Elliott! Does it feel good to have absolved yourself of blame for our break-up?'

The hand that lay on his knee clenched into a fist and she could see from the whitened knuckle the strain that he was having to keep his control. He breathed deeply and then she saw him force himself to relax. 'There's no point raking over the ashes,' he said harshly. 'Our marriage is dead and buried and we both admit as much. It was an unfortunate mistake on both sides. We all make them sometimes.'

'I'm glad to hear you admit it. I was beginning to think that you considered yourself infallible these days.'

'You can be sure of one thing, Cassandra,' he informed her tautly. 'I learn by my mistakes and I never make the same error of judgment twice.'

She shrugged and feigned thankfulness. 'I'm relieved to hear it. I'd hate to have to fight you off. I hear husbands sometimes get possessive when they see their wives with other men.'

'Not this one. Please yourself as far as I'm concerned. I shall certainly be doing so while I'm here.'

A sudden pang went through her at the thought of Elliott taking another woman to replace her. It was silly, really. She could hardly expect him to have lived a life of celibacy since the last time she had seen him. In fact he'd admitted that he'd been playing the field. Did she genuinely imagine that he might have been struck by remorse because his wife had caught him entertaining another woman in the flat that they had shared together during their married life? That was not only naïve, it was unrealistic in the extreme. But whereas what she didn't know about she was prepared not to dwell upon and even to be happy in her ignorance, the prospect of seeing Elliott with another woman, perhaps wining and dining her, charming her under Cassie's very nose, was an unpleasant one.

'Shall we get back to business?' he enquired, more intimate topics, such as failed marriages, having apparently lost their interest for him. 'Pleasant though it is trading insults with you, Cassandra, we have clients to meet and a full day ahead of us.'

'Certainly,' she said through clenched teeth. 'And I'd be grateful if we restricted our discussions to work in future. I don't like wasting my time on fruitless conversations.'

'I think that could be arranged,' he responded. 'It might save wear and tear on both of us.'

She would hardly have been surprised if she had stalled the car instead of starting as smoothly as she did, but all went well and it did not take long to reach the small hotel in the Boulevard Georges Clémenceau where the Coxes were waiting for her. Introductions were effected and the elderly couple were installed in the car. Mrs Cox, a pleasant woman, somewhat younger than her husband, shared the front seat with Cassie while Mr Cox and Elliott took the rear of the car. It was no small relief to Cassie to have her husband's presence removed from her side, although she had the feeling that there was every chance, despite his assertion to the contrary, that he might become an irritatingly critical back-seat driver.

They crossed the Rhône and drove southward across the flat expanse of marshland towards the coast. Here the evidence of the modern tourist invasion became apparent with ranches and inns catering for those who wished to have riding holidays, but still have access to the night life to be found in the nearby resort towns. Cassie pointed out the signs offering horses for hire, explaining as she did so the dangers of trying to explore the swampy land without the help of one of the *gardiens*, the expert horsemen of the area, who are familiar with every inch of the ground and treat the shifting, treacherous bogs of the region with great respect.

'I've got three properties to show you that may suit your needs,' she told the Coxes. 'They're all about the same size. The one we're heading for at the moment is a small, whitewashed farmhouse, one of the kind that you've been seeing all along our route. Its owner had it converted for use for holiday lettings, but he's getting on now and doesn't want the bother of it all, so he's decided to sell up.'

'And the others?' Mrs Cox asked.

'They're in Les Saintes-Maries-de-la-Mer, otherwise known as *Li Santo* in the local Provençal language. At one time it was just a peaceful fishing village, but now the tourists have discovered it in a big way and it's become much livelier. You may feel less isolated there than in the depths of the countryside.'

She drew up at the farmhouse and they got out with appreciative murmurs at the picture made by the contrast of the sturdy, white building against the brilliant blue of the sky. Even this early in the morning the sun was blazing down. It was pleasantly warm now, but soon it would be almost unbearably hot.

Cassie led the way to the door and unlocked it for them. 'The house is empty,' she told the couple, ignoring Elliott's tall figure as he brought up the rear. 'Would you like me to come round with you or would you rather wander round on your own?'

They elected to look round the place for themselves. 'No offence intended, my dear,' Mr Cox explained apologetically. 'But quite often you're so busy listening to what's being said about the place that you don't really have the chance to study it properly.'

'That's quite all right. I understand,' she smiled, and
only regretted giving them the choice when she realised
that it would leave her on her own with Elliott.

'You don't believe in the hard sell, then?' he enquired as she stood anxiously wondering what to say.
Until now, by absorbing herself in the job at hand, she
had managed to blot out his presence on the trip with a
fair degree of success, but now he had obviously decided
it was time to step in again and make his existence felt.

'No, I don't.' She bridled instantly. 'I think you can
push people too far by doing that. I want them to be
entirely happy with the house they choose, not end up
buying something they don't like because of high-
pressure sales talk.'

He leaned casually against the wall of the house and
felt in his pocket for some cigarettes. He offered her the
packet and she shook her head, waiting while he lit one
for himself with lazy deliberation and drew on it
heavily before answering her. 'I see. Do you find that
you sell many houses that way?' he asked.

'I find that in the main I usually manage to sell
houses to people who are satisfied with them long after
they've signed the contract.'

'Very laudable. But you haven't answered my question, have you?'

'I haven't had any complaints about my sales
technique,' she said. 'Do you think you could do any
better?'

'Possibly not. I don't have your obvious assets.' His
eyes lingered over her figure, making it all too clear
what he meant.

'People don't buy houses on the strength of an attractive face or a good figure,' she said contemptuously. 'If
you think they do, it shows how little you know about
the subject.'

'*People* don't, but I'm sure *men* do,' he stressed unpleasantly. 'And I'm sure you do everything you can to encourage them.'

'With their wives looking on? Come off it, Elliott. I'd have to be a darned sight more subtle than I am to pull any tricks like that. And, for what it's worth, although I don't suppose you'll believe me, Mr Thompson warned me against getting involved with the clients when I first came out here, and I've followed his advice.'

'I can imagine. Did he want you all for himself? I wonder how he felt when you ditched him in favour of his office boy.' He stubbed out his cigarette savagely and she got the impression that he would have liked to have crushed her with equal violence.

'Why, you—you——!' she stammered with rage, incapable of finding words strong enough to hurl at him.

'Are you going to try to slap my face again?' he asked. 'It's amazing how you react to a few home truths. You will remember what happened last time, won't you? I'd hate you to bite off more than you could chew.'

She restrained herself with difficulty from hurling herself at him in a seething, kicking temper, the like of which had not seized her since nursery days. But she stopped herself in time. It would do no good to let him goad her into attempting anything of the sort. He would only enjoy watching her make the effort.

'Are you being deliberately crude and unpleasant or is it just another part of your nasty nature that you managed to conceal from me while we were enjoying married life?' she enquired coldly.

'What do you think?' He straightened up and moved towards her.

'I think you're despicable, Elliott Grant!'

'Nice to know that I'm appreciated,' he said, and reached for her.

What his intentions were, she did not know, but she could make a shrewd guess at them from the pattern of their last encounter. With a strength that she did not know she possessed she evaded him. 'I'll go and see if the Coxes need any help,' she announced and, brushing quickly past him, stumbled into the house and slammed the door behind her.

CHAPTER FOUR

LET him think what he liked about her behaviour; she
was past caring. She leant back, breathing heavily,
against the solid wooden door and closed her eyes
wearily. At least he didn't seem to be making any effort
to follow her, which was just as well, because she didn't
feel she would have the energy to prevent him if he
tried. She was conscious of the hot tears pricking behind her eyelids and fought them hard. She was a fool
to let Elliott get to her emotions in this way, she told
herself. What did it matter that he so obviously despised her? Did his good opinion of her really count for
anything at all?

Evidently it did. He still had the power to hurt her
and he was using it mercilessly, taking every opportunity to criticise and take her to pieces. She supposed
that he was getting some kind of enjoyment out of the
process. Perhaps by pointing out that her morals were
less than lily-white he was excusing his own lapses. Or
could it be that he just got a twisted pleasure out of
running her down now that he had no further use for
her himself?

One thing was certain: she had every intention of
keeping out of Elliott's way in future. It didn't matter
in the least if he noticed and chalked it up as a victory
to him. Her peace of mind was more important to her
than any childish triumphs in battles of wits between
them. Out of business hours there would be no problem and she supposed that Jules and Mr Thompson
would prove adequate bulwarks against him at the
office. But, on occasions such as today, when she would

have to cope with him on her own?

She smiled mirthlessly. What was she worrying about? After Elliott's pointed remarks about her sales tactics she wasn't even sure that she'd have a job after today. If he had his way she might be out on her ear and looking for work elsewhere. He was quite ruthless enough to take that step, she was sure. Or perhaps, if he was kind enough to leave her job intact, he would see to it that she was never allowed out with a client again, merely left to concentrate on the typing and filing and other paper work.

She heard the tramp of shoes on the bare wooden staircase that led down from the small loft area and forced her worries about Elliott to the back of her mind. For the moment, at any rate, she had people to look after and whether these were the last clients she ever dealt with or not, she intended to devote as much care and attention to them as usual.

'I was just coming to make sure that you'd seen everything,' she said, giving the couple a bright smile as she walked towards them. 'These farmhouses were originally built only as one storey, but, as you can see, the present owner converted the loft space into a spare bedroom or attic. He had the window put in too. It's a wonderful view out over the marshes and reed beds on a clear day like this.'

'No need to go out tramping after the wild life,' Mr Cox joked. 'I could see it all from up there.'

Having established that they had seen enough, Cassie led them outside, her heart pounding agitatedly at the sight of Elliott's tall figure standing by the car. All traces of anger had disappeared from his face and his expression held only the right amount of polite concern for their clients and their welfare. He ignored Cassie.

They got into the car again and headed for the sea, the Coxes enthusing happily about the sight of a troop

of creamy-white horses not far from the roadside and a
distant glimpse of herons flying over one of the small,
reed-fringed lakes. Occasionally they passed clumps of
trees, pines and cypresses planted to serve as wind-
breaks, but mostly the landscape offered a botanist's
paradise of marsh-loving plants, tamarisks and all kinds
of reeds, grasses and flowers.

'A bit desolate,' commented Mrs Cox, although her
husband did not agree with her, and she brightened
considerably at the sight of the cheerful little fishing
village which was their next stop.

Elliott hovered in the background as Cassie escorted
the couple round the first of the two properties they
had come to view, listening with apparent interest to
what she had to say.

'A little poky,' was Mrs Cox's brief verdict after they
had seen the tiny-roomed cottage and emerged from the
dimness within to the dazzling light of the street outside.

Cassie didn't argue the point as perhaps she might
have done out of Elliott's cramping presence. With
him there her usual skill in dealing with people seemed
to have deserted her, and, nice though the Coxes were,
she could summon little enthusiasm for the task in
hand. The faint look of disapproval which crossed his
face at her responses to a couple of questions from Mrs
Cox made her jumpier than ever and she found herself,
albeit unwillingly, glancing towards him to gauge his
reaction to everything she said.

He made no comment, but the decisive way that he
took charge as they approached the second house was
criticism enough.

'I'll take the keys, Miss Russell,' he said smoothly,
and his tone brooked no arguments. 'I'll do the honours
this time.' He held out a hand and she surrendered the
heavy key-ring to him, hating him as she did so. Did he

have to humiliate her in front of their clients by making it quite clear he found her totally incompetent? He would be apologising for her next!

He escorted the Coxes to the door and opened it, ushering them inside with a pleasant smile. But the look he turned on Cassie as she made to follow was cold.

'There's no need for you to come round with us,' he told her, and shut the door practically in her face. She had no option, but to remain outside. Unless she decided to make a scene, of course. And he knew perfectly well that good manners and professionalism would prevent her from doing that in front of outsiders.

She supposed drearily, as she waited for them to reappear, that he was employing whatever sales talk he knew in an effort to get them to buy the property. It was attractive enough with its stone walls and deep, sloping roof, but hardly the most restful of places in the summer months when the streets of the village were thronged with chattering tourists. And, compared with the cool spaciousness of the farmhouse they had visited, the small cottage rooms looked cramped and claustrophobic to Cassie's eyes when she glanced quickly through the window.

Elliott would have a job on his hands convincing the Coxes that they would be happy there. She wondered how he, a financier more familiar with the varied vocabulary of the Stock Market, would cope with the very specialised jargon of the estate agent's selling pitch. Badly, she hoped. It would be good for him to realise that he couldn't do everyone's job as well as he undoubtedly performed his own. It might teach him a valuable lesson.

But, from the smile on his face when they emerged from the doorway of the fisherman's cottage, it seemed that her hopes were to be frustrated. He had the look of a man who had been successful in an undertaking and she hated him for it, as he led the older couple over to her.

Mrs Cox had been less than thrilled with the isolated situation of the farmhouse and the second house they had seen, but couldn't have been more delighted with this place. 'It's absolutely perfect,' she enthused. 'The ideal layout and the ideal situation. It's just what I've been looking for.'

Cassie tried to respond enthusiastically, aware that Elliott was listening with a slightly sardonic look on his face to every word she uttered. He was perfectly conscious of the fact that every polite praise stuck in her throat because it was a tacit acceptance of the good job he had done on the sale. No doubt he was feeling a righteous satisfaction at having proved to her that even the worst houses on their books could find a buyer, if they were projected in the right way.

She wondered what kind of confident spiel he had come up with to talk the Coxes into buying, sure in her own mind that it was Elliott's charm, applied with a trowel, that had influenced Mrs Cox. After five minutes in his company the older woman would have eyes only for the assets which he pointed out, rather than the disadvantages of the place which he would have skated over quickly, if at all. How could he?

She made a point of turning to Mr Cox who had been content to let his wife voice her enthusiasm, but had remained silent himself. 'Are you happy with this cottage, Mr Cox?' she asked, stressing the pronoun slightly. 'Don't feel that we're pressurising you to buy something that you're not certain about. Take your time about deciding.'

Elliott cut in with a quick frown. 'I think they know their own minds, Miss Russell,' he said, giving her a warning look that boded ill for a later date.

She defied him openly, knowing that there, at least, Elliott had no power to stop her. He could hardly use physical force on her to ensure her silence in front of her clients. 'Mr Grant is from head office,' she explained with an innocent smile. 'He doesn't usually come out with us on our viewing trips and, naturally, he doesn't realise that——'

'A pity you can't add him to your sales team. He'd be a first class man in the field.' Mr Cox, the very person who had voiced his dislike of high-pressure salesmen, defended Elliott instantly. Did the man brainwash people into approving of him? Cassie wondered. The older man had clearly misunderstood the drift of her remarks and was trying to reassure her. 'No need to worry about not coming round with us, my dear. Mr Grant made a wonderful job of showing us the place. We really saw its potential as a home for us.'

'I'm sure you did,' Cassie replied with an edge to her voice.

Mr Cox turned to Elliott and grinned broadly. 'It must make quite a change for you to get away from the board meetings and the like and have the opportunity of driving round the countryside with a pretty girl, eh?'

Elliott's expression did not indicate that he particularly enjoyed the experience. 'As you say, it makes a change,' he said politely, and was swift to change the subject. 'If you've seen everything, perhaps we should be heading back to town.' He glanced at his watch. 'You'll be wanting some lunch, I expect.'

'Perhaps you'd care to share some lunch with us here, by way of a small celebration?' Mrs Cox asked tentatively, and her husband seconded the invitation with enthusiasm.

'A good suggestion. We can't thank you enough for finding us just the place we wanted and we'd be de-

lighted if you'd join us. It seems a bit flat to drive
tamely back without cracking a bottle or two to com-
memorate the occasion of finding our ideal retirement
home.'

'It's extremely kind of you both, but——'

Elliott seemed on the verge of refusing when a per-
verse streak in Cassie prompted her to interrupt him
and accept the invitation on his behalf as well as her
own. 'What a good idea! We'd love to have lunch
with you, wouldn't we, *Mr* Grant?' She gave him her
sunniest smile, challenging him to deny the fact and
knowing full well that there was no way he could do so
and still seem polite.

His look at her held a quick blaze of anger that she
should presume to direct his actions, but it was quickly
masked as he turned to the Coxes. 'We should really be
getting back to the office, but——' He shrugged and
capitulated gracefully.

'What the lady says goes?' Mr Cox enquired archly.
He seemed absolutely determined to embarrass Cassie
by imagining a close, extra-office relationship between
herself and Elliott. She wondered how she would get
through lunch if he intended to keep this up through-
out the meal.

Elliott seemed not a whit disturbed. 'Don't the ladies
always get their own way?' he asked. 'But on this occasion I'm only too happy to fall in with their wishes.'
He included Mrs Cox in his mocking glance. 'Shall we
find a restaurant before they become too crowded in
the midday rush or whatever the Provençal equivalent
may be?'

He indicated that the Coxes should precede them
and took Cassie's elbow in a vice-like grip as they
followed the older couple down the narrow street that
led to the main part of the village. She tried to wriggle
free, but his hold on her only tightened.

'Elliott, let go of my arm,' she begged him in an undertone. 'You're hurting me.'

'Good. That's nothing to what I'd like to do to you at this precise moment,' he said with quiet fury. 'You deserve a good hiding, and if I had you on my own, you'd be getting one right now.'

She laughed bravely and reminded him, 'You did say that you were only here as an observer today. You can hardly blame me for taking the initiative.'

'Is that what you'd call it?'

'Don't you want to celebrate your first success in your new career as a salesman?' she taunted him. 'Or is it beneath your dignity as owner of the company?'

His eyes narrowed with anger, but his tone, as he replied, was pleasantly conversational. 'Be careful, Cassandra. You'll regret it if you make me lose my temper with you.'

'I didn't think I was capable of making you do anything,' she said airily. 'That's a new departure for me, at any rate.'

'I'm warning you——'

She was spared the necessity of replying by the Coxes, who had found a small pavement café on the other side of the street and were waving them over to it. Cassie was relieved at the interruption. Arguing with Elliott brought a heady excitement akin to dicing with death, but she was aware that in a sustained battle between them only a fluke could give her a victory over him.

They found a table out of the direct rays of the sun and sat down, ordering, on Cassie's recommendation, a huge meal of Provençal specialities, starting with *tapenade*, an hors d'oeuvre of pounded olives, fish and capers, served with crusty French bread.

The Coxes were in a high good humour and their constant flow of conversation disguised the fact that their guests responded to them, but addressed each other in tones of arctic politeness.

Mr Cox was full of praise for Cassie's help with the menu and the fluent French in which she addressed the waiter as their plates were removed and replaced with the main dish she had chosen for them, *filet de porc*, marinaded in wine, herbs and garlic, and accompanied by the locally grown rice.

'You shouldn't be wasting your time showing old folk like us around houses,' he told her freely. 'You should be married with a home of your own and a husband and children to fill it.' In sudden doubt he glanced at her hand, verifying that she wore no wedding ring. 'I don't know what the young men you know can be thinking of not to snap you up.'

'Brian!' his wife protested in some confusion. 'Stop it! You're embarrassing the poor girl.'

'I'm sorry, my dear. All I meant was that it wasn't natural for someone as pretty as Miss Russell to be left on the shelf.'

'Oh, it takes more than just a pretty face to keep a man happy,' Elliott observed. 'But I expect you realise that, don't you, Cassandra?'

She dodged the issue neatly, refusing to rise to the taunt and saying with a shake of her head, 'Perfectly true. You're difficult creatures to please, I'll grant you that. We poor females offer you perfection in human form and you have always some reason for complaint.'

'I don't think you'd have much difficulty in pleasing any man,' Mr Cox said with heavy gallantry.

'I understand that her admirers queue up for the pleasure of being tossed aside.' Elliott had an unpleasant glint in his eye.

She was not going to let his deliberate baiting of her make her angry. 'That's right,' she agreed. 'I always tell myself that I'm only young once, so I might as well make the most of it. Why not have two strings to my bow?' She gave a wicked smile. 'Or three. Or four. Or even more.'

Elliott joined in the general laughter that greeted her sally, but she noticed his hand clenched on the table top and a slightly forced note in his voice. She speculated as to what might be annoying him now. Was it merely the fact that she showed no indication that his gibes were getting to her? Or did it go deeper? Could Elliott be jealous of her supposed male admirers? She dismissed the idea as quickly as it entered her head. A man who had made it clear that fidelity in marriage meant nothing to him could hardly have grounds for complaint if his wife decided that what was sauce for the goose was sauce for the gander. And after five years she could scarcely be expected to live like a nun. She gave a half-smile, wondering what his reaction would be if she told him the truth—that there had been no one in her bed since the last time he had shared it with her.

Mrs Cox was teasing her now. 'And you haven't found one man good enough to settle down with out of all these dozens?'

'I'm very choosy.' Cassie laughed and refused to be drawn further on the subject. 'Time will tell. I'll invite you to the wedding when it happens,' she said mischievously. Let Elliott think there was someone else that she cared about, if he chose to take it that way. It might do him good to be made to accept that she had a life of her own now in which he no longer figured. Perhaps his pride might take a well-deserved knock at the thought that he had been replaced in her affections without any difficulty. He wouldn't like that. He wasn't accustomed to taking a back place.

The talk veered away from the personal, much to Cassie's relief, as the young, dark-eyed waiter came over to take their empty plates and receive their compliments on the food with the air of one who expected no less. They finished the wine and sat replete, sipping coffee and cognac and watching the world pass by.

'In the summer the place is thronged with holiday-makers,' Cassie told them. 'And also for one occasion earlier in the year. People flock here in May to see the great gathering of the gypsies. According to legend the saints after whom the village is named landed here from Palestine to preach the Christian gospel. Their servant was an Egyptian called Sara and her remains are buried in the church here. She became the patroness of the gypsy tribes and they come here from all corners of the earth to honour her once a year.'

'It sounds fascinating.' Mrs Cox was intrigued. 'Well, we'll be able to witness it for ourselves next year.'

'That is, if we manage to tie up all the details of the sale for you successfully.' Elliott seemed determined to bring the pleasant interlude to an end as soon as possible and revert to business matters. 'This has been most enjoyable, but I'm afraid we must drag ourselves away and get back to work.'

Had he been so single-minded, so dedicated, when she had known him before? Perhaps that side of him had always been there, but he had chosen not to reveal it to her. After all, you didn't get from nowhere to Elliott's current position in life without driving yourself hard. There would be no time-wasting on the way. Cassie wondered where a blonde named Liz and the other ladies who had flitted through his life slotted into the pattern. Perhaps they had been less demanding than she had been on his time. And even Elliott couldn't work for twenty-four hours in every day ...

'I'd rather like to look round the place and get my bearings a little. Maybe take another look over the house, if that's possible,' Mrs Cox asked. 'I was hoping that we could spend the afternoon here as well.'

'We'll get a taxi back later in the day,' her husband said, understanding better than she did the demands of business life. 'Obviously we can't expect you to hang about with us. If you're agreeable to letting us have the keys, we could drop them off at the office later and sign any necessary documents at the same time, if that's all right.'

'Fine.' Elliott wasted no words trying to change their minds, merely handing them the keys from his pocket. 'We'll see you later this afternoon. Are you ready to leave, Cassandra?' He turned an unsmiling face to her.

Her heart sank at the prospect of the drive back to Arles with no friendly couple to act as buffers between herself and Elliott. On the journey out she had been able largely to ignore him, but she somehow doubted whether it would be possible to do that on the return trip. What would she do if he saw it as an opportunity to mete out retaliation for her behaviour towards him? She would be the first to admit that it had been slightly out of line for an office junior to take towards the man who ran the whole show, but surely there were extenuating circumstances? Looking at her husband's set face Cassie didn't somehow think that he would be taking those into account when he considered the matter.

There was no reprieve. The faint hope that the Coxes might change their minds about staying for the afternoon due to sudden weariness or an opportune cloudburst died almost immediately. The sun mocked her with its brightness and warmth and the Coxes looked disgustingly refreshed after their extended lunch break. They waved a cheery goodbye after thanking Elliott again for his help and disappeared into the crowds which thronged the main street. She was on her own with Elliott and she wished that she hadn't drunk so much wine to give her Dutch courage over lunch. She

should have realised that she would need all her wits
about her.

He noticed, of course. It was too much to expect that
he hadn't. When they reached the place where she had
parked the car he held out his hand for the keys.

'I'll drive. I didn't indulge as heavily as you did over
lunch.'

'Are you implying that I'm drunk?' she demanded.

He gave her a withering look. 'If you're not, you're
well on the way to it and certainly in no condition to
drive a car.' He detached the keys from her nerveless
fingers and gave her a none too gentle push in the
direction of the passenger side of the car. 'Get in and
don't argue,' he said impatiently. 'I've taken about as
much as I'll stand from you today.'

She obeyed him, because there seemed no point in
not doing so. In the mood he was in he was quite capable of seizing her and thrusting her bodily into the
car. She gave a studiedly nonchalant shrug and climbed
in.

Elliott did not ask her for directions and she volun-
teered none, staring resentfully straight in front of her
as he unerringly took the right route for home. He
glanced at her a couple of times, but said nothing,
apparently unwilling to break the state of armed
neutrality between them.

He drove in silence for a quarter of an hour and
Cassie had begun to cherish the hope that the journey
might be completed in this way, when he said, 'There's
no need to sulk, Cassandra.'

'I'm not sulking,' she answered, still not looking at
him.

'It looks rather like it to me. You haven't said a word
since we left the village.'

'Silence is golden, didn't you know that?' she said
rudely. 'Anyway, what were you expecting me to do—

compliment you on your superb sales technique?'

'I had to do something,' he pointed out with infuriating mildness. 'You were well on the way to letting them go without buying anything. McIlroy and Wentworth is supposed to be a paying concern, you know.'

She shrugged. 'I don't like harassing people into buying. I don't care for sales that are made dishonestly.'

'What was dishonest about it?' He was looking at the winding road ahead, not at her, as he spoke. If she had not known him so well Cassie might have suspected from his casual tone that he was not really interested in defending himself. But she noticed the way the strong brown hands suddenly tightened on the wheel and knew that her crack had gone home. But his voice was eminently reasonable as he told her patiently, 'The Coxes saw the second cottage. They liked it. And they've decided to buy it. As far as I'm concerned, that's the end of the story.'

'I wonder if they'd have liked it half so much if you hadn't insisted on going round with them, pointing out the advantages and making light of the drawbacks to the place?'

'Have you ever heard the expression *caveat emptor*?' he enquired softly. 'It means, let the buyer beware. It isn't my job to act as surveyor for our clients. That's up to them. I'm in the business of selling houses.'

'I thought you employed staff to do that for you,' she snapped at him. 'While you sit counting the profits at head office. Or does it give you a kick to step down from the heights of Olympus occasionally and see how the lesser lights in your organisation are managing?'

'If they're all as sensitive as you about accepting help when they need it, I hardly think there would be any profits for me to count,' he commented drily.

'What makes you think that they wouldn't have bought anyway? You really do have an inflated opinion of your talents, don't you?' she snapped. 'I didn't need any help.'

'Didn't you? You know perfectly well that you'd never have made a sale this morning if I hadn't stepped in. But you haven't the courage to admit it, have you? And now you're accusing me of using every dirty trick in the book, because you can't bear the fact that I've just demonstrated that I can do your job better than you can.'

A bird flew low across the road in front of them and the car swerved slightly as he registered its presence.

'Watch what you're doing,' she said irritably, reacting too quickly. 'I'd like to get home in one piece, if you don't mind.'

'In that case I won't try to concentrate on two things at once,' Elliott replied, and, swinging the car off the road, he brought it to a halt on the salt-cracked earth that surrounded them. 'Not that I can guarantee your safety even then, of course, if you keep on with the tack you're taking at the moment,' he added nastily.

She felt suddenly nervous of him. 'What are you doing?' she asked.

He killed the ignition and turned in his seat, stretching one arm casually along the back of the head rest, and looking as if he had all the time in the world to waste. 'You've been spoiling for a fight ever since I arrived here, haven't you, Cassandra? Well, now's your chance. We're not likely to be interrupted and we have,' he consulted his watch, 'at least two hours, maybe longer, before anyone at the office will start wondering where we've got to. Fire away.'

She stared at him blankly. She had always mistrusted him in one of his sweetly reasonable moods. With some men, perhaps, such a tone indicated a patient, understanding nature. With Elliott it meant only the calm before the full fury of the storm was unleashed on the head of anyone who dared to oppose him.

'I thought work was important and couldn't wait? You certainly gave the Coxes that impression,' she said.

'I never consider getting to know what makes my staff tick as a waste of time.'

'I'd scarcely have thought that you needed to apply that process to me. I'm your wife.'

'You were my wife,' he corrected in his turn.

She did not reply, merely turning her head away from him and studying the flat landscape beyond the car with apparent interest.

'Look at me, Cassandra,' he commanded, but she ignored the order.

The touch of his lean, strong fingers under her chin, forcing her to face him, sent a tremor through her, although she could not have said whether it was one of excitement or apprehension. But Elliott was always sure of prompting a reaction from those with whom he came into contact. He was not a man to be viewed with indifference.

'I always thought,' he said pleasantly, 'that you'd be a stunningly attractive woman when you'd outgrown the childish tendency to throw temper tantrums and fits of sulks when someone got the better of you.'

'And I always imagined that you'd improve when you'd learnt that you weren't lord of all you surveyed,' she retorted, not to be outdone. 'It seems we were both fated to be disappointed.'

'I wouldn't say that.'

His hand had moved to the base of her throat and his thumb was stroking her skin caressingly. She could feel the tiny, throbbing pulse at the side of her neck leap into life at his touch. Not for the world could she have shaken off his hand, although her stirring senses warned her that now was the time to draw back.

'Changing your mind about my talents, Elliott?' she

asked. It was an effort to get the words out as a sudden breathlessness seized her.

'They were never in question,' he said, and, pulling her towards him, he kissed her.

She could not help but respond. He set-her senses alight with tingling pleasure, his touch making the world spin dizzily and fade away to insignificant nothingness. All that mattered was the firm pressure of his mouth against hers, the feel of his arms sliding round her to fold her closer to him, the knowledge that he was still attracted to her.

His kiss deepened and she clung to him, responding mindlessly to the pleasure which he aroused in her. Waves of sensation flooded through her and she muttered a half-protest as his lips left hers and blazed a burning trail down her throat to explore the shadowy promise of her breasts.

She felt his hands undo the buttons of her flimsy blouse and made no attempt to stop him as her body warmed to his expert lovemaking. She was drowning, lost in a flood of hectic delight, careless as to the consequences, but only aware that she did not ever want him to stop what he was doing to her.

The continuous blare of a car horn penetrated her consciousness a few seconds after his. With a sudden expletive he broke away from her. In a daze Cassie was aware of a small red Fiat flashing past them, its driver's hand still on the horn and its occupants, four youngish men, turning to look back at the parked car, cheering derisively at Elliott and herself.

He laughed roughly, although she had the feeling that he did not find it funny. 'We certainly seem to have made someone's afternoon. I wonder if those were cries of envy or of solidarity?'

Cassie felt as if he had suddenly slapped her. The moment was gone, shattered into a thousand pieces at the sound of the hard mockery in his voice. Shakily she eased herself into her corner of the front seat and forced her shaking hands to fasten up her blouse. It took several attempts and, although Elliott was looking at her and well aware of her difficulty, he made no move to help her.

'I've no intention of apologising for that.' His voice held a note of contempt, but whether it was directed at her or himself for giving in to a momentary weakness, she had no idea.

'Did I ask you too?'

'I'm sure you would have done as soon as you came down to earth.'

She had recovered her senses in the moment that he had thrust her aside, but her one conscious thought had been the wish that he would take her in his arms again and resume the passionate lovemaking that had been so rudely interrupted. But she had no intention of telling him so. Not now that she realised that the moment had meant nothing to him.

He seemed to guess what was running through her mind and gave her a look charged with mockery. 'You'd been asking for that all day. No, don't deny it,' he said as she opened her mouth to counter indignantly. 'You wanted it as much as I did.'

'Perhaps I wanted to make comparisons,' she said savagely. 'And give you the chance to do the same. So you admit that I still hold some attraction for you?'

His jet-dark eyes scanned her and this time she met his scrutiny boldly. 'Do you expect me to deny it? We may have had difficulty in communicating on most levels during our married life, but in that area at least we were always—compatible.' His gaze flickered over her, as if marking the physical changes since they had parted. Then he said deliberately, 'Still, there was scarcely time for us to tire of each other, was there?

You ran out on me long before there was any danger of that happening.'

'And now you're making up for lost time, I suppose?'

'You could say that.' He considered the question. 'You're a very beautiful woman and you go to a man's head like wine. My brain may tell me to despise you for all you've done, but my senses offer me a different story. I still want you,' he said crudely. 'Your body turns me on as much as it ever did. Satisfied?'

Did he expect her to be after what he had just said? He made her feel like a cheap adventuress who cared for nothing except pleasing her own appetite for physical love and who exploited her talents in that direction in order to get exactly what she wanted. She was cut to the quick, but she fought desperately not to show her hurt to him. He would only glory in the fact that his words had struck home. Well, if his opinion of her was so low, she would try not to disappoint him.

'I've proved my point, Elliott. You're like all the rest—vulnerable to any desirable woman who happens your way. And I thought once that you were made of sterner stuff than that.'

'No woman's ever made me do something I didn't want to do. Bear that in mind before you start congratulating yourself,' he said sardonically. 'You failed last time round, remember?'

How could she ever forget? The humiliation that had come with her realisation that she was not capable of holding his affection had hit her hard. That and the memory of the good times with Elliott had been her chief reasons for not trying again with any one of the many likeable men who had approached her. She supposed that at the back of her mind there had always been the hope that some day she would triumph over that humiliation or at least find the reason for it. That, perhaps, she and Elliott might meet again and be reconciled. Now she knew what an adolescent pipe-dream that had been. To Elliott she was no more now than she had ever been to him: a beautiful, desirable woman who attracted him and whom he wanted to possess. There had been no more to their marriage than that. She felt suddenly sick.

'I don't admit defeat very often these days,' she said proudly.

'You may find you have to where I'm concerned.' Even the angle of his dark head displayed arrogance.

'We'll see, Elliott, shall we?' was all she said in reply.

CHAPTER FIVE

THEY completed the journey back to Arles in a stony silence. When they reached the office Cassie jumped out almost before the car had stopped in her haste to get away and have at least a moment's respite from Elliott's suddenly hateful presence.

'What's up?' Jules asked, raising his head from the pile of papers on his desk, as she stormed in and slammed the door behind her.

'Does anything have to be the matter?'

'No. But when you come in after a day in the company of our revered Elliott Grant with a face that would turn milk sour, you can't blame me if I assume that something's happened between you. Do I assume that you had a good day, then?'

She grimaced. 'No, you certainly do not! Or to put it another way, everything that could go wrong did go wrong, and he seemed to think that I was responsible.' She sat down at her desk and surveyed the pile of paperwork awaiting her attention with despondency.

'*Pauvre petite*. He gave me a rough ride too, if that's any consolation. I spent most of the night lying awake devising horrible, lingering deaths for him. Boiling in oil is too good for that one.'

Cassie gave a reluctant laugh. 'Idiot,' she said, knowing that he was trying to cheer her up and appreciating the attempt. 'Is that your idea of helping me cope with the problem?'

'If the problem's Elliott Grant, there's no way I can solve it.' He laughed. 'I admit defeat there. But if it's just a question of arming you for the battle with him,

I can suggest various solutions.'

'Such as?'

He smiled at her. 'Have dinner with me tonight and I'll boost your morale. I'm not as hard to please as some people obviously are.'

About to shake her head and turn down this offer as she had refused him on several previous occasions, Cassie paused as a noise behind her indicated Elliott's entrance into the office. Suddenly she was seized by a childish impulse to demonstrate to him that she had a life of her own now, of which he was no longer any part. She was free to choose her own friends, who had nothing to do with him; to go out with men who found her attractive and made no secret of the fact, but not in the obvious way that Elliott had just done, telling her crudely that he lusted after her still.

'Thanks, Jules,' she replied, smiling at him. 'I'd love to come out with you tonight. It'll make a pleasant change to be with someone civilised—I've had enough of boorish men today.'

Jules sent her a quick, warning look and seemed about to launch into speech, when an icily cold voice forestalled him.

'Edifying though your opinions are, Miss Russell, I'd be glad if you'd keep them to yourself. I believe I mentioned it to you before.'

She turned and simulated a start of surprise at seeing him. 'Why, Mr Grant. I didn't realise that you were listening.'

'I could hardly help it,' he said pointedly, making it clear that he had seen through her little act. 'But you knew that, didn't you?'

'I——' She floundered helplessly, at a loss for a smart answer.

He glanced over at Jules who was listening with interest. 'Have you no work to do?'

'Plenty, thank you.'

'Then I suggest you get on with it,' Elliott snapped and, striding across the room, opened the door to Mr Thompson's office without knocking, and closed it behind him with a firmness that indicated his mood all too clearly.

Jules gave a low whistle of astonishment. 'What's biting him?' He glanced at Cassie in sudden comprehension. 'Or need I ask?'

'He had a bad day too,' Cassie told him briefly.

'That I can see, although I can't imagine why. Didn't you manage to charm him?'

'I didn't try. He's immune.'

'Surely not,' he protested in disbelief.

'We rub each other up the wrong way. We——' About to say that they always did, Cassie broke off guiltily. Nice though Jules was, she had no intention of trusting him with the story of her marriage. There were some things that it was better to keep private.

Jules had not noticed her hesitation and continued, 'The man's mad, that's what I think. But I'm not complaining. All the less competition for me.'

'Who says you need worry about the competition?'

'I do. It's taken long enough to get you to come out with me.' He looked fairly aggrieved. 'Most girls would leap at the chance.'

'I do like a modest man,' she teased him. 'And anyway, I'm not most girls. And I'll thank you to remember that.'

'There's no need to remind me. I've been sitting across from you every day long enough to realise that.'

He had a serious note in his voice and Cassie felt a pang of misgiving. Was it fair to use Jules just to get one over on Elliott? She had always despised women who played off one man against another for their own ends. And now she was doing it herself.

'It is only dinner,' she stressed. 'There's no need to read anything significant into it, you know.'

'Of course not. But after an evening of experiencing at first hand my handsome features, my sparkling wit and my dazzling conversation, I could hardly blame you if you fell at my feet and begged me to make passionate love to you.'

She laughed. 'Forewarned is forearmed,' she told him. 'I don't think there's any danger of that.'

Cassie found herself looking forward to the evening ahead as she let herself into the house that evening and took the stairs to her rooms two at a time. At least she would not be sitting at home brooding about Elliott and his strange attitude towards her.

For the rest of the afternoon he had been constantly in and out of their office. If she had not known better she would have said that he could not bear to let her out of his sight. But that could scarcely be the case. He had made it all too apparent that she was no longer his responsibility. Perhaps she was reading too much into it and he was merely making sure that the two office juniors did some work instead of giggling together as he clearly thought they employed most of their time. Mr Thompson had never tried such tactics, she thought indignantly. But then Mr Thompson was easy-going and friendly. And Mr Thompson was human, not an uncaring, cold automaton like Elliott.

Cassie took off her neat, office clothes and, donning a robe, went to the bathroom for a shower. Soaping herself under the cool, reviving spray, she told herself that she let things get to her far too easily. When the Coxes had called in as they promised to confirm the purchase of the cottage, she had grown more and more resentful of what she considered to be their fawning respect for Elliott and his opinions. Most women would have ignored their manner. Most would have kept their tempers when their estranged husbands baited them.

Most women would have—— But she was not most women: she had told Jules as much.

A faint smile touched the corners of her mouth as she towelled herself dry and went to inspect her wardrobe to select the dress she would wear to go out that evening. Jules had denied it vigorously, but she knew perfectly well that, like all the other men who had asked her out, he was hoping that this evening would lead to other outings and sooner or later to a more intimate relationship. And he would be wrong. It might lead to the sort of complications that she would prefer to avoid at the office. But Cassie dismissed the worry even as it occurred to her. She could handle Jules. He wasn't like Elliott.

She scanned her dresses critically, wondering where Jules would be taking her, and finally decided upon a sleeveless green linen with a low neck, severely cut and styled, but suitable enough for the most elegant of restaurants. She had a faint suspicion that he might try to impress her by taking her somewhere luxurious.

She gave herself a light make-up, applying green eye-shadow with a sparing hand and outlining her mouth with a dash of coral lipstick. She surveyed the result in the mirror of her dressing table and wished for the hundredth time that her skin would take a tan instead of growing, if anything, more translucent in the heat of the sun. It seemed almost as if her vitality had drained from her face into her hair, which glowed like rich copper and shone with life as she drew the brush through its rippling waves. She debated whether to leave it loose, falling softly to her shoulders and framing her fine-boned face and high cheekbones. Elliott had liked it that way, delighting in running his fingers through the springy curls and creating a riotous disorder that had taken ages to untangle. Not that she had cared about that. Not then.

She frowned at the memory and pulled a box of hair-pins towards her. What Elliott had liked then need not concern her now and she would do well to remember the fact. She pulled her hair into a smooth chignon and secured it with the pins. That was better. She was no longer the alluring siren that Elliott had called her in those early, happy days of their marriage. She was a cool, poised woman, confident and sophisticated and entirely in control of herself and her destiny. She pulled a face at the reflection in the mirror and wondered who she was fooling.

She found her black evening bag, sprayed herself with a little of her favourite floral perfume and, snatching up a lacy shawl in case it grew cool later on, she went downstairs to await Jules' arrival in a mood of pleasant anticipation.

'Off out with your young man?' Madame Martin enquired as she and Cassie almost collided at the foot of the last flight of stairs.

'A young man, certainly, but he's not my exclusive property,' Cassie smiled.

'He won't have eyes for anyone else the way you're looking tonight, *ma petite*.' Her landlady studied her approvingly. 'And it's about time that you went out and enjoyed yourself. You're too young to stay in night after night. It's not natural.'

'You'd rather I went out painting the town red and then woke you in the early hours of the morning by clattering drunkenly up the stairs?'

'You wouldn't be the first tenant who's done that. Nor the last, I imagine,' Madame Martin told her philosophically. 'I was the same at your age, so I can understand.'

'I'm sorry to be such a disappointment to you, *madame*,' Cassie said demurely. 'But I do enjoy being on my own, you know. I like reading and sewing and listening to my records.'

'Reading indeed!' The elderly Frenchwoman raised her eyes to the heavens and gave an expressive shrug. 'You'll have time enough in plenty to do that when you're my age and the men no longer queue at your door.'

The doorbell sounded sharply and, laughing, Cassie went forward to open it. 'I'll try not to disappoint you, *madame*,' she called back, and smiled a greeting for Jules.

'What was all that about?' he asked suspiciously as he took her arm and seated her in his small open sports car. 'Was she urging you to ignore my wicked wiles?'

'Quite the contrary,' Cassie told him. 'She was telling me to make the most of them.'

He laughed. 'She sounds like a sensible woman to me. I'll have to see what can be arranged along those lines.'

It did not take long to reach Jules' choice of restaurant. As she had suspected, it was elegant and impressive, attracting a well-dressed, chic clientele, drawn mainly from the town's more prosperous citizens, but with the odd tourist, seeking a change from the restaurants of the four-star hotels. The dining room was airy and spacious with doors at one end which gave on to a garden whose fragrant flowers scented the room with their differing perfumes. At the windows lacy curtains stirred slightly in the warm night air. The silver on the white tablecloths gleamed in the subdued, but effective, lighting.

It was the perfect setting for a romantic dinner *à deux* and something akin to a pang of regret shot through Cassie at the thought that she was not sharing an evening with someone who meant more to her than Jules. But she dismissed the regret quickly, feeling guilty. Jules had been kind and considerate enough to think of bringing her to this beautiful place and giving him a pleasant evening now that they were here was the least that she could do.

She smiled at him as the waiter led them to a small table, discreetly tucked away in a secluded bay, and seated them, returning an instant later with menus for them.

'You like it here?' Jules asked, already anticipating her answer.

'Mm. It's superb. I've never been here before.'

'Good. I should not like you to be dwelling on other happy times on our first evening together.'

'The first? You seem very sure there'll be others,' she said softly.

'But of course. How could you think otherwise? I never abandon a beautiful woman after only one date.'

She ignored the compliment. 'I might abandon you.'

'You would not be so unkind.'

'No?'

'No,' he told her firmly, reaching across the table and taking her hand. 'You have a soft heart, Cassie, for all your fiery temper.'

She pulled her hand away. 'You're no gentleman to refer to my temper,' she reprimanded him with mock severity. She turned her attention to a study of the menu. 'Have you been here before? What would you recommend?'

He followed her lead and entered into a spirited discussion of the dishes available. In the end Cassie took his advice and opted for a starter of fresh, raw vegetables, accompanied by a spicy, garlic sauce, followed by *loup de mer*, a variety of local fish, grilled and flavoured with fennel. She leaned back in her chair after surrendering her menu to the waiter and glanced around her with interest while Jules buried himself in the wine list. It was really a superb place to eat. If the food lived up to the promise of the elegantly decorated dining room with its rich-piled carpet and creamy textured walls, hung with old Provençal prints, it would be a memorable evening indeed. Idly she studied the other diners, wondering if anyone she knew was likely to be there. This was just the sort of place to appeal to a few of their clients who might choose it for an evening out. It needed no flashy gimmicks to boost its reputation, only its own quiet excellence of atmosphere.

Her eye was caught by an attractive blonde in a severely cut, obviously couture black dress, which fitted her generous curves as if moulded to them. The slender black shoulder straps only emphasised the pale honey colour of her bare shoulders and accentuated the platinum sheen of her long, studiedly disarranged hair. It took time and money to achieve that effect of stunning simplicity, Cassie thought, and wondered if her escort, or rather husband, she amended quickly, seeing the wide gold wedding band matched with a large, glittering diamond on the same finger, fitted in with the general air of sophistication about her. So often, Cassie discovered, women of her type of full-bodied glamour selected mates who were fat, balding and generally unappealing. Perhaps money conquered all other instincts —or possibly they deliberately chose men who would offset their glamour even more by contrast.

The woman moved slightly in her place, affording Cassie an excellent view of her dinner partner as she did so and making her suddenly wish that she had directed her attention to some other part of the room. She gave an involuntary gasp as she stared straight into Elliott's jet-dark eyes. They held a cool, faintly sardonic expression as they met hers and she surmised that he had registered her presence in the restaurant before she had noticed his. He raised a quizzical brow and then inclined his head slightly in curt recognition of her.

The blonde woman noticed the action and turned to look at the object of his attention. With one all-embracing glance she summed Cassie up and summarily dismissed her as a force to be reckoned with and then bent her interest to Elliott again, leaning towards him in a curiously intimate way and murmuring something to him.

Cassie heard his laughter in reply and wondered if the remark had concerned her. The other woman had made it plain that Cassie presented no form of threat to her evening with Elliott even if he had deigned to acknowledge her. She wondered if he would bother to explain who she was, and then decided that the office junior did not merit such consideration. And she felt strangely rejected at the thought of him dismissing her from his mind so easily.

'Cassie! Cassie? Have you gone into a trance?' Jules was trying desperately to gain her attention and she gave a start and came back to earth suddenly.

'Sorry. I was miles away.' She debated whether to tell him that Elliott was here and decided that it was only fair to do so, even if it ruined his evening too. Jules was unlikely to commit any major indiscretions, but it was probably better to warn him, just in case he felt like trying to dance on a table top or drink himself into a stupor.

'Elliott Grant? Where?' he asked.

'Over there.' She pointed them out to him.

'Oh, well,' he shrugged. 'It's a nuisance, but it can't be helped. It's a free country and I suppose he's got a right to dine wherever he likes. It's just inconvenient for us that he happens to have fixed on this place. But from the look of things I think he's too occupied with his glamorous dinner date to pay much attention to what we get up to.' He appraised the blonde with a Frenchman's usual eye for an attractive member of the opposite sex.

'Who is she?' Cassie asked curiously. 'Do you know her?'

'By sight and reputation only. She is Michèle Durand. Her husband was Charles Durand, a wealthy industrialist, who retired here about five years ago after making a pile in Paris.'

'Was?'

'He died about eighteen months ago. The word is that Madame Durand would not be averse to finding a successor to him. And this time she'd like someone nearer to her own age. She found an ailing, tiring husband, some twenty-five years older than herself, a little tiresome at times, so they say. Although I suppose one must admire the lady for sticking by him until the end.'

'And inheriting his fortune?'

'Alas, no. Oh, it was so very sad.' Jules looked amused. 'Despite all her care and devotion to him, the old gentleman was not grateful. He left her the house in which they had lived near Aix-en-Provence and an annuity that would be enough for most people to get by on if they lived reasonably economically. The bulk of the estate went to his children by his first wife.' He laughed. 'I understand that when the will was read the air was blue with her responses to it!'

'So she's on the look-out for a wealthy husband now?' Cassie asked, summing up the situation pretty quickly. Designer dresses didn't cost peanuts.

'I imagine so. She is a practical lady, *tu comprends*, and it would be the practical solution.'

'Then she could ensure that she kept up the same standard of living. Do people still do that sort of thing?'

'Evidently they must. I wonder if she has our Monsieur Grant lined up in her sights?' said Jules.

'Oh, surely not!' She was curiously reluctant to contemplate the idea.

'Why not? He's rich. He's attractive. What more could a woman want?'

'Surely most women would want some degree of loving in such a relationship?'

'*Chérie*, you are a romantic and I applaud you from the bottom of my heart. But Michèle Durand does not think like that. She is a realist. She realises that love will not pay the rent. And our Monsieur Grant must seem a very good proposition compared with some of the men that she has been forced to contemplate.'

'I wonder where she met him.' Cassie voiced her thought.

'She's thinking of selling her house. It's big for one person and she cannot afford the staff to keep it up at the moment. We called there to inspect it the other day when Elliott Grant was out with me. She seemed fairly taken with him then.'

'And did he like her?' She could have kicked herself for asking the question, but somehow she had to know.

Jules gave a cynical smile. 'Let us say that he appreciated what she had to offer.'

'And now they're having dinner together.'

'And so are we, if you remember. And we've spent quite enough time discussing Elliott Grant. I thought that you'd have been eager to get away from him after what you've told me of your day together.'

'I would have been.' Cassie pulled a face. 'But he's rather hard to ignore when he's only just across the room.'

'Forget him,' Jules instructed. 'He's not important. Outside the office we meet on equal ground. He is no longer the boss. *Bien,* so we will disregard him.'

She laughed. 'Easier said than done! But I'll try.'

And, to a certain extent, she succeeded, by forcing herself to pay attention to her companion's easy chatter, which ranged over a vast number of subjects. On another occasion, away from Elliott's presence, which was casting such a shadow over her evening, she might well have enjoyed herself immensely. But it was an effort to project an air of happy unconcern when she was all too aware of the grim glances that Elliott cast in their direction every so often, almost as if he felt that they should have retired from the scene once they had observed his presence there.

'What's the matter, *chérie*?' Jules asked as she pushed aside the greater part of her main course uneaten. 'Didn't you like it?'

'Oh, yes,' she assured him. 'It was delicious. But I wasn't very hungry and the portions here are huge.' She could hardly attribute her lack of appetite to the fact that the man across the room put her off her food, which was the real reason.

She managed to eat a bowl of fresh salad and cream for her pudding and attempted to laugh and joke normally as she sipped her coffee. She seemed to be making a reasonably good job of it, for Jules responded happily and appeared not to notice the inner tension which she was sure must be written all over her face. Still, it could not be long now before they left the restaurant. Jules had only to settle the bill and then they could go. It was a little early perhaps, only just after ten o'clock, but she could plead tiredness and get him to take her straight home.

But it seemed that Jules was under the impression that the evening's entertainment was just beginning. As she drained her coffee cup and looked at him expectantly, thinking that he would call the waiter over and ask for the bill, he smiled at her with the air of one who has a great treat in store. He waved over to the far end of the room and she saw with a sinking heart that a group of musicians had appeared and were preparing to play.

'You would like to dance?' It was a statement, rather than a question. He would clearly be offended if she said no.

Weakly she gave in without attempting to get out of the situation. She did like dancing. Perhaps out of sight of Elliott she could lose herself in the music and enjoy the experience. She got to her feet, took Jules' outstretched hand and let him lead her over to the space that had been cleared for a dance floor. Fortunately their route between the tables did not take them past Elliott and his lady friend, but Cassie was conscious of her husband's eyes following her progress the length of the room. He seemed determined to ensure that her evening was ruined, she thought bitterly.

She was not surprised when, a couple of dances later, Elliott and Michèle Durand joined the crowd on the dance floor. She had an idea that Michèle would display herself to advantage there, and in that she was not disappointed. They were a spectacular couple. Cassie was not the only one whose head turned to look in their direction. Michèle, a sinuous figure, swaying expertly in time to the music, had eyes only for her partner and Elliott, in an expertly tailored evening suit with a crisp white shirt that set off his tanned skin, looked darkly handsome and was easily the best-looking man in the room. He was a good dancer, responding to the music with natural rhythm and easy grace. Cassie had often marvelled how light he was on his feet for such a big man.

Over Jules' shoulder Cassie's eyes followed them until they were lost to sight at the opposite end of the dance floor. Then and only then was she able to return her attention to her partner, who, mercifully, did not appear to have noticed that her mind had been elsewhere.

'Enjoying yourself?' Jules asked her, and pulled her closer to him, kissing her lightly on the cheek as he did so.

She edged cautiously away again. 'Of course,' she lied. 'It's been a wonderful evening.' Out of the corner of her eye she could see Michèle's blonde head pressed close to Elliott's dark one. Hastily she averted her gaze and pressed her cheek against Jules' shoulder, feigning obliviousness to anything and anyone but him. That would show Elliott how much she cared about him and the other woman in his life, she decided defiantly. If, of course, he was capable of dragging his eyes off Michèle for long enough to notice what Cassie was doing.

She started and missed her footing when his voice suddenly broke in on her thoughts. 'Good evening, Pinot. Are you enjoying yourself?' He sounded as if it was costing him an effort to be polite. 'You don't mind if I deprive you of your partner for this dance?' Then, without waiting for Jules' reply, he had prised her away from the young Frenchman and had taken her in his arms, whisking her deliberately away as if she had no more will than a rag doll.

She was stunned into acquiescence for a few startled seconds, then made as if to get away from him. 'How dare you?' she said furiously. 'Let me go at once!'

His grip on her tightened, resisting her attempts to free herself from him. 'Don't be stupid, Cassandra,' he told her softly. 'You can't have a row with me in the middle of the dance floor in front of all these people. Give in gracefully and the ordeal will be over quicker.'

She turned her head, looking anxiously back for Jules.

'Oh, don't worry about him,' said Elliott, reading her thoughts with ease. 'You'll be restored to him sooner or later. Whether it's sooner or later rests with you.'

'All right,' she gave in, as she had known that she would even as she started fighting against him. 'I'll dance with you, although I really can't understand why you want me when you've got a perfectly good partner of your own.'

'I like variety,' he said coolly.

'And what does your glamorous partner think about that?'

'Michèle?' He glanced down at her, one corner of his mouth quirking slightly with some emotion that she could not identify. Amusement? Satisfaction? Cassie did not know. 'Oh, you noticed her, then?'

'One could hardly fail to in that dress,' she retorted. 'Every man in the place was ogling her.'

'Careful! Your claws are showing. Jealous, Cassandra?'

She gave a studiedly casual laugh. 'Good heavens, no. You can use your charms on anyone you please. It's no longer any concern of mine.'

'Is that why you've been studying us so earnestly all the evening?'

So he had noticed the glances that she had darted at him, thinking herself unobserved. She ignored the question and commented, 'I didn't know that you liked blondes. You never used to.'

'My tastes have changed since you knew me,' he said, making it quite clear that whatever relationship they had shared, it was definitely in the past tense. His arm tightened round her as they negotiated a crowded stretch of the dance floor. Then he continued, 'But then I wouldn't have thought that Jules Pinot was your type, and look how wrong I am.'

Instinct nearly prompted her to utter the denial that hovered on her lips, but pride stepped in to save her just in time. 'Yes, he's a very different sort of man from you,' she agreed. 'But I'd hardly make the same mistake twice, would I?'

His lips compressed firmly and a tight look of anger came across his face. 'He obviously hasn't had any greater success at teaching you a few manners.' Roughly he pulled her closer to him, despite her frenzied efforts to resist him, and moved with her purposefully towards the wide doors which led on to the garden.

One minute they were in a mass of people on the crowded dance floor and the next they were on their own in dim, sweetly-scented air outside. But this was hardly the time to appreciate the quiet charm of the place. Elliott was still holding her in a vice-like grip, and Cassie's attention was entirely taken up with the problem of how to free herself from it.

In desperation she aimed a sharp kick at his shins and had the satisfaction of knowing that it had gone home from the muttered expletive that was forced from him.

'Damn you, you little vixen! Do you never accept when you're beaten?' he asked furiously.

'It takes more than brute force to shut me up.'

'Really? Then I'll have to try other methods of persuasion, won't I?' His head bent towards hers and she knew what his next action was going to be.

'Let me go, Elliott, or I'll scream,' she warned him.

'Scream away,' he said indifferently, and kissed her full on her unwilling mouth.

There was no point in struggling, her tired brain told her, as he plundered her lips in the old well-remembered way. Better by far to give in and let him do his worst. But Elliott's worst was an insidious invasion of her senses, rekindling a flame within her that had never really died in all the years of separation.

She responded to him in the end. It was inevitable that she would do so and only a matter of moments before she gave him the satisfaction of knowing that even now, at odds with him on almost every other level, she was capable of forgetting all she hated about him and losing herself in a world of illusory pleasure.

As he felt her struggles to be free of him abate, his hold on her slackened slightly, allowing her arms the freedom to creep around his neck, one hand caressing the dark, springy hair that grew low on his collar. His movements were gentler now, as he roved over her body possessively, stirring her to an even greater response. His mouth left hers to nibble the lobe of her ear and she moved against him in sudden delight at the action.

'Cassandra, you little witch,' he muttered feverishly as he pulled her down, unresisting, on to one of the stone benches with which the garden was ornamented.

His hands were at her hair now, dragging the confining pins away with a fierceness that made her wince with pain and mutter a faint protest as he pulled at them. The last pins scattered to the floor and he was fondling the long, silky strands, wrapping them round his fingers as his mouth returned to tantalise her senses with its hard pressure on hers.

She was dimly aware that she should not be allowing him to sweep her literally off her feet like this. What was happening to her? Had she lost a will of her own? Why didn't she tell him firmly that his lovemaking meant nothing to her any more? Because she would be lying through her teeth if she did, her drugged mind told her. As his fingers found the zip at the back of her dress and slid it down to send shivers of delight racing through her spine at the touch of his hand on her bare back, she knew that she no longer wanted to stop him.

She moaned with pleasure as he slid the dress from her shoulders, shivering slightly at the feel of the cool night air on her bare skin. But then she no longer noticed anything but the feel of him, caressing and arousing her to a peak of excitement as his hands roamed freely over her firm breasts, their flimsy covering yielding to the urgency of his desire for her. She was aware of his hard need of her, although he was keeping a check on himself, restraining his ardour even as he stirred her to delight.

But it was still a shattering shock when he tore himself from her, saying in a thick voice that she hardly recognised as his, 'Your boy-friend will be coming looking for you if you don't get back to the dance floor soon.'

'Jules!' She breathed his name in a sudden realisation of what she had so nearly done. How could she have let one man nearly make total love to her out here in the garden, when her escort for the evening was inside, awaiting her return with impatience? She felt suddenly cheap.

Elliott had recovered his usual poise and was standing surveying her flushed face. 'Unless,' he said pleasantly, 'you want him to come out here and catch you looking like the little slut that you are. No? I thought you probably wouldn't. You'd better tidy yourself up then.'

He waited with obvious impatience as she made a valiant effort to pull herself together and mend the havoc that he had wrought with her appearance. There was nothing that she could do with her hair without the aid of a mirror, and anyway she had lost half the pins and couldn't see where they had fallen to in the half-light. She contented herself with running a comb through her hair and hoped that it would serve. Then, restored to a semblance of her normal self, she turned to her husband.

'It might be better if we didn't go back together,' she suggested with an attempt at coolness.

He shrugged. 'If you like,' he said. 'Enjoy the rest of the evening.'

How dared he say that, as if nothing of any importance had happened between them? But she presumed that from his side of the fence, nothing had. He had merely chosen to teach her what he regarded as a well-needed lesson. Now, having delivered it, he would ignore the consequences to the girl to whom he had administered it.

She glanced round to tell him as much in stinging tones, only to find that he had taken her at her word and gone back into the dining room. Presumably Michèle would be waiting for him like a well-trained lapdog. Damn Elliott, she thought viciously, although whether she was lashing out at him for what he had done to her, or the fact that he had abandoned her to return to another girl, she was uncertain.

There was a noise behind her and she tensed. Had Elliott thought of some other insult to fling at her and returned to deliver it in person? Then she relaxed as Jules' voice came through the darkness.

'Cassie? Are you out here?'

'Yes. I'm by the wall.' Her brain tangled with the problem of what explanation to give him for her behaviour.

'I was concerned about you when I saw Elliott Grant back with Michèle and you nowhere to be seen.'

So he had not seen Elliott coming in from the garden. She breathed a sigh of relief. 'I had a bit of a headache,' she told him. 'I thought that if I got a bit of fresh air I might feel a little better.'

Jules was all solicitude and she felt a heel for lying to him. The only consolation was that he would have been even more upset if she had told him the truth. 'Do you feel any better?' he asked, concerned.

'I feel absolutely terrible,' she said with brutal honesty. 'Would you mind if we went home?'

CHAPTER SIX

FORTUNATELY Jules asked no further questions of her.
If he had noticed her pale, strained face, the bruised
look about her eyes and the sudden vulnerability that
showed itself in the set of her mouth, he did not look
further to account for them than the reason that she
had given him.

He slipped a comforting arm around her shoulders.
'Of course I'll take you home. Why didn't you tell me
before that you weren't feeling very well?'

Because the onset of her 'illness' had coincided exactly
with her first glimpse of Elliott's arrogant features
across the room from her. And she could hardly have
expected to get away with that. What kind of construction would he have put on the fact that she could
not endure their boss's presence in the same room, out
of office hours? She had no intention of telling Jules
and finding out.

She pressed her hand to her brow, which, despite the
coolness of the night, was flushed and lightly dewed
with perspiration. Why had she let herself get into such
a state over Elliott? He was only a man, after all,
human and fallible like all the rest that she had met.
What was it about him that fired her blood and made
her react like this? Jules had accused him of acting
as if he was a lord of creation, but tonight he had been
more a prince of darkness, a devil sent to tempt and
beguile her to destruction by playing on her baser instincts. And how easily he had succeeded in his mission!

'Is there another way out of here without going back
through the dining room? I can't bear that crush of

people in there,' she told him, desperately seeking to avoid another encounter with Elliott at all costs. Who knew what nasty digs he might make at her in Jules' presence, while she felt weak and quite incapable of replying to them with any competence. Anyway, she did not want to give him the satisfaction of seeing her retreat from the field of battle and concede victory to him by so doing. Let him spend a while searching the room in vain for her until he realised that she had gone.

'Of course, *chérie*. There is a side door. I have paid our check, so it will be all right if we slip away quietly. Can you manage to walk or shall I carry you to the car?'

She attempted to raise a weak laugh at his exaggerated air of concern. 'It's only a headache, Jules. I'm not going to collapse on you or anything like that.'

But all the same, she was glad of his supporting arm as they walked slowly across to the small wooden door in the garden wall and went through it to the car park beyond. Jules seated her in the passenger side, fussing over her to such a degree that she was ready to scream at him to leave her alone and just drive her home as quickly as he could. She bit back the words with difficulty and gave him a small, forced smile of thanks instead. It wasn't his fault, after all.

He drove carefully back into the centre of town, as if he were transporting a crate of eggshells. To Cassie the journey seemed interminable, although it could not have taken more than ten minutes. When they reached her door, he got out to help her and insisted on taking her key and unlocking the door for her.

'You will be all right, Cassie?' he asked anxiously, his brown eyes still concerned. 'Is there anything at all that I can do?'

She shook her head. 'No, nothing, thanks. I'm sorry to have spoiled your evening like this.'

'Not at all,' he denied with conviction. 'I have enjoyed myself. It is you that I am sorry for. But there will be other times, *n'est-ce pas?*'

She felt even more guilty for her actions that evening. 'Yes, of course,' she agreed hastily.

'And now you must go and rest.' He bent forward and his lips brushed her cheek in a gentle, affectionate gesture. '*A demain, ma mie.*'

'Yes. I'll see you tomorrow.'

She closed the door on the sight of his departing figure and dragged herself wearily up the stairs that she had come down so lightheartedly a few hours earlier, looking forward to the evening ahead. She would have been a little less eager if she had known what had been in store for her. Thank goodness Madame Martin had not taken it into her head to lie in wait for her and enquire after the success of the outing. That really would have been the last straw.

She opened her own door and went straight to the bathroom to find some aspirin and a glass of water. The fictional headache was fast becoming a reality. That would teach her to tell lies! Gulping down the cool, reviving liquid, she caught sight of her reflection in the small mirror above the wash-basin. Her hair was still wildly disordered despite her efforts to comb it into some semblance of respectability. Her face was pale, but her cheeks had a hectic, unnatural colour and her lips, devoid of lipstick now, had a ripe redness that owed nothing to artifice and a good deal to Elliott's hard possession of her mouth. She thought that it must be obvious to anyone who saw her that she was a woman who had been thoroughly kissed and who had surrendered herself totally to the experience. How could Jules have been so unperceptive as to accept her glib lies as the truth?

Cassie undressed and prepared herself for bed, sure,

as she put out the light and lay there in the darkness, that she would not sleep after all she had been through that evening. But, surprisingly, in the middle of reliving the moment when Elliott had appeared and whisked her off to dance with him, his dark face bent over hers like a hawk intent upon its prey, she fell asleep.

It would have been better, perhaps, to have tossed and turned, sleepless all night long, than to have experienced the dreams that came to her then and left her drained and unrefreshed when she awoke the next morning. She was in an enormous ballroom that sparkled with the lights of thousands of candles, hung from the ceiling in cut glass chandeliers, which glittered and shone in the mirrored walls of the room. She was with Jules and they were on their own, dancing to the sounds of a Strauss waltz played by an unseen orchestra, whirling together in perfect harmony, their bodies twisting and turning in response to the rhythm of the music. She watched their reflected images in the glass as they skimmed by. Every way she turned her head she could see herself and her partner, carefree and happy.

Then the picture suddenly changed and when she looked back at the man she was dancing with he had suddenly turned into Elliott. An Elliott whose face was a dark mask of anger and contempt for her. In her dream she could feel his arms around her, bruising her with the force with which he held her, forcing her to follow his lead as they circled the room. He was talking to her, saying hateful things about her, and she could not respond and repudiate them. It was as if she had suddenly been struck dumb. Her mouth kept opening and shutting, but no sounds would come out. And Elliott seemed totally unaware of her difficulty, shouting at her as if expecting her to answer him back. She shook her head desperately from side to side in an effort to alert him to her plight. But he did not care.

Cassie woke up shivering and clutching herself. The bed was in a shambles with her duvet on the floor and the pillow somehow tangled up in the undersheet. She looked wildly around her, almost as if she expected her husband's figure to emerge from behind the door, then gave herself a mental shake and got up to make herself a pot of tea. Usually she followed French custom in the mornings and had a large cup of coffee or chocolate with her breakfast rolls. But today she felt in need of a strong, bracing cup of tea. It had always been her mother's panacea for all ills, and as she sipped the hot liquid gratefully, Cassie had to admit that she felt a little better.

It was strange how every problem always seemed to look bleakest at night, she thought. In the bright sunlight of another perfect Provençal summer day the cares of the previous evening diminished slightly in proportion. Although they still loomed appallingly large, she had more hope of finding a solution to them. She poured herself another cup of tea and, after liberally spreading a *croissant* with butter and peach preserve, she took them through with her into the sitting-room and attempted to review the situation.

Elliott's behaviour was the completely unknown factor. Jules knew nothing of what had happened between them the previous night and Cassie at least had no intention of enlightening him. But might Elliott tell him out of sheer bloody-mindedness? There was no other reason why he should: someone in Elliott's position would normally think it far below his dignity to meddle with the personal affairs of his office staff. But this was scarcely a normal situation, although Jules did not know that, of course. As far as he was concerned Elliott's views mattered only in one area: that of the office. He would deeply resent it if Elliott tried to interfere in his private life. But suppose Elliott justified his reasons for doing so? Suppose he explained that Cassie was his wife?

There was no reason for him to do that, she reassured herself quickly. He had already accepted the fact that she had not mentioned that she was a married woman and always used her maiden name when he addressed her. She had assumed that he, too, found it more convenient to forget that they were still legally bound to each other. That he did not want reminding that they had shared anything.

No, Elliott would not say anything. The malicious pleasure to be gained from the act would be more than balanced by the disturbance it would cause in office relations. Cassie's spirits lifted as she showered and dressed in a floral smock dress, one of the prettiest that she owned. It gave her the look of a demure schoolgirl and, although she had donned it because it was the first thing that came to hand, she was well pleased with the effect when she glanced in the mirror. Suitably chastened, that was what Elliott would assume when he saw her.

Strangely, she did not stop to consider Jules' reaction. And the thorny problem of why, exactly, Elliott had behaved the way he had the previous evening, she ditched completely until she had more time to consider it. When she had recovered a little, perhaps her bruised feelings would allow her to look at the matter dispassionately. For the moment the most important thing was to encounter him with coolness and dignity at the office this morning. Her hand went to her make-up bag and she worked quickly and skilfully at blotting out the dark shadows under her eyes and the general air of lassitude about her, assuming a sophisticated front, rather at odds with her dress. Still, it would have to do.

When she walked into the office, her head held high, Elliott was nowhere to be seen and she was almost disappointed that, having made the effort, he was not there to witness it.

'You're feeling better this morning?' Jules sprang to his feet and crossed the room towards her.

'Much better,' she assured him. 'I really don't know what came over me last night.'

He shrugged. 'These things happen. We cannot order them. I will take you there again some day soon and you will enjoy yourself this time.'

At the moment Cassie felt that she would be glad if she never set eyes on the place again, but she supposed that the reaction would pass. 'That's a date,' she said, trying to sound cheerful.

They learnt from Mr Thompson that Elliott would be out for the morning.

'I understand that he has gone over to see Madame Durand about some details connected with the selling of the property,' the older man told them.

'Convenient for him,' Jules muttered in an undertone. 'I wonder if he did drive out there this morning or just decided to get up late and take a late breakfast with the lady as he was there already?'

The thought had crossed Cassie's mind, too, but she pushed it aside. She found that she did not like the idea of Elliott spending the night with the sensational-looking Frenchwoman. Was it possible that he had gone straight from making passionate love to Cassie to do the same to Michèle? Was he capable of doing such a thing with cool calculation? She supposed bleakly that he was.

Mr Thompson was clearly glad of a morning to himself. He looked almost as if he had been reprieved from execution at the thought of a few hours' respite from his superior's demanding presence and disappeared into his office after telling Cassie that on no account was she to disturb him with phone calls or visitors.

'Unless it's Mr Grant, of course,' he added hastily.

'Of course,' Cassie assured him gravely. 'I won't forget.'

Jules smiled and stretched lazily. 'Safe for a while. A few hours free of the man. Just like old times, isn't it? It's hard to imagine that he's only been here for a few days. I feel as if we've all aged at least twenty years under his exacting rule.'

'Poor Mr Thompson takes the most stick,' she said sympathetically. 'He has to put up with him all day long, sharing his office. He's been made to work harder than I expect he's ever done. He's walking on eggshells all the time, poor man.'

'His cronies at the Coq d'Or will be wondering what's happened to him,' Jules agreed. 'No long lunch breaks these days. Well, we'll survive, I suppose.'

'You don't sound very sure about that,' Cassie teased him, suddenly relaxed at the thought of postponing the confrontation.

'Maybe he'll mellow as time goes by.'

'Optimist!' she laughed. 'I wouldn't count on it.'

And when, after lunch, Elliott finally favoured the office with his presence , it seemed that she was right not to expect him to be in a good mood. The outer door slammed to behind him with a decisive thud and caused a draught which scattered papers everywhere. About to comment, Jules glanced at his employer's set face and thought better of it, merely going down on his hands and knees to pick up the mess from the floor. Elliott ignored them both and went into the inner office.

Jules cast her a speaking glance, but said nothing. With Elliott obviously in a bad mood, it was probably best for them to keep their heads down and wait for the storm to pass over. At least, thought Cassie, typing furiously as she composed a list of properties newly on the market, Elliott had not taken the opportunity to unleash his temper on her. She wondered if he was still brooding about last night or if something else had caused it. Perhaps Michèle had registered displeasure at being abandoned in favour of an office junior and had taxed him with it? It was never wise to nag Elliott, as Cassie knew to her cost. Not that anything had stopped her trying!

Mr Thompson was sent out like an errand boy rather than the man nominally in charge of the Arles office in order to show a married couple around a new block of apartments on the coast. He clearly thought the assignment beneath his dignity and was protesting as much as the door opened and Elliott escorted him through the outer office.

'I usually send Monsieur Pinot or Miss Russell to attend to these things. I've trained them both myself and I've always found their work excellent.'

'That's not my experience after going out with them,' Elliott replied calmly, ignoring the fact that he was in their presence. 'Perhaps it's about time that you re-freshed your memory on the selling side, Thompson.' There was a faint gleam in his eye and Cassie wondered what was coming next. 'Take Pinot with you. Perhaps, between you,' he added sarcastically, 'you might man-age a sale for once.'

'Yes, of course.' The older man would have agreed to anything to get away from the lash of Elliott's tongue and Jules looked glad to escape too.

The door closed behind them with a finality that made Cassie aware of her position. She was alone in the office with Elliott and completely at his mercy. She felt a cold shiver go through her as she heard the Citroën start up outside and drive away, as if abandon-ing her to her fate. Had he arranged it deliberately? She buried her head in the house list again, hoping that he had returned to the outer office, although a prickle at the back of her neck warned her that he had done no such thing. Unable to bear the suspense any longer, she turned her head and looked at him.

He smiled. A cruel, taunting smile, as if he was looking forward to watching her struggling impotently to get the better of him when he held all the winning cards in one hard, lean hand. She was suddenly afraid. Elliott was her husband and, five years ago, she thought that she had known him as well as it was possible ever to know another person. But she had not really understood him then, and now she felt as if he was a total stranger despite his familiar features.

'I'm sorry to drag you away from such pressing business,' he drawled. 'I'll see that you get back to it as soon as possible. But first you and I have got some talking to do.'

'Have we?' she asked. 'I wasn't aware of it.'

'You thought what happened last night was over and forgotten?'

'It is over,' she stressed. 'And I'm trying to forget some parts of it at least.'

'Would that be the time that you spent with Pinot or the episode with me?'

She looked at him deliberately, temper suddenly replacing her fear of him. 'What do you think?' she said.

His eyes narrowed as he looked at her. 'I didn't notice you responding to him the way you did to me. Or was that reserved for later, after he drove you home? Tell me, did you go to his place or yours? Or weren't you too bothered about the locale?'

There was a white, pinched look about his mouth and she had the impression that he was driving himself to throw insults at her. He wanted her to lose her temper, but for once she was not going to. She would keep her cool and see how he liked that.

'Does it matter?' she answered coolly. 'If the man's the right one for you, the place isn't important, is it?'

'And Jules Pinot is right for you? Don't make me

laugh,' he said savagely. 'He couldn't handle you in a thousand years.'

'And you could, I suppose? How do you propose to go about it, Elliott? You try to railroad over everything, don't you? You married me thinking that here was someone young and naïve enough to be easily moulded to your will. And you got a shock, didn't you? Well, I'm no easier to handle now than I was then. So why not admit it?'

His hands clenched by his sides and, for a split second, Cassie wondered if he would lose control and if Jules and Mr Thompson would find her lifeless body slumped over her desk on their return. Elliott looked furious enough to commit murder just now.

'I thought I gave you a fair demonstration of my ability to deal with you last night,' he said tautly.

She gave what she hoped was a casual shrug. 'You're an attractive man—I've never denied it. It was a momentary lapse, if you like.'

'I see. And does he satisfy you, this boy lover of yours?'

'Is that any of your business?' she asked sharply.

'If I choose to make it so. For all your new-found independence and reversion to your maiden name, you're still legally tied to me, Cassandra.'

'Tied is the operative word,' she snapped. 'But our marriage vows don't seem to have meant very much to you in the last five years. You haven't been exactly pressing in your attentions towards me.'

'Better late than never.'

'Do you really think so? I was beginning to think that I'd never see you again.'

'Did you want to?' he asked.

She paused before she answered him, aware that physically Elliott still had the power to stir her senses. She looked at him and registered again the fact that whereas five years ago he had been a good-looking man, now he exuded a virile masculinity and confidence that could leave few women unaware of him. But she had learnt by bitter experience that physical attraction was only a part of what was needed to hold two human beings together in a successful marriage. Now she knew better than to trust the quickening of her pulse rate when she was with him.

'Surely you were too busy being a success in the City to think about me?' she said with a touch of bitterness. 'I suppose I should have learnt that lesson at my mother's knee. It was a pity that I forgot it when I married you. Business deals always take precedence, don't they?'

'Sometimes,' he allowed. 'It depends what competition they're up against.'

'In my case obviously not strong enough to present any serious threat to your concentration. Poor, trusting fool that I was! I never realised that others might succeed where I failed.'

He tensed. 'You've only yourself to blame for that.'

'Because I didn't fight back? Where would that have got me?'

Elliott dismissed the question, frowning. He started to speak again and then was silent.

'Have you run out of excuses?' she taunted him.

He gave her a direct, searching look. 'Would you have welcomed me, Cassandra, if I'd made the effort and met you halfway in an attempt to patch things up?'

She was surprised. Had it ever occurred to him to try? She rather thought not. How would she have felt if he had come to her in those first agonising months after she had left him? When the sight of a tall, broad-shouldered figure with Elliott's walk in front of her in the street had made her quicken her step until she had assured herself that it was not he. When she had spent sleepless nights tossing on her narrow bed at her parents' house, her mind on other nights that they had spent, passion-locked in each other's arms. She had ached then for the touch of his hard body against hers, arousing her and taking her to heights of desire that only he could show her.

If he had approached her then, would she have rushed back into his arms? Would she have forgiven him for being unfaithful to her? She did not know. And now it was too late to dwell on what might have been all those years ago. Now her attitude had changed, hardened against him. She did not need Elliott any more, she told herself. She could stand on her own feet.

'No,' she said, looking straight into his handsome face and hoping that she convinced him.

She hadn't. 'Are you certain about that, Cassandra? You don't sound as if you are.' His eyes were running casually over her slim yet shapely figure. Was he remembering the way it had come alive under his touch last night?

She managed a short, derisive laugh. 'What's the matter, Elliott? Can't you take no for an answer?'

'Forgive me,' he said ironically. 'You weren't saying it too loudly last night, as I recall, were you?'

She could not deny it. 'Your behaviour last night only convinced me how right I was to put you out of my life. I'm sorry if your masculine pride won't allow you to accept the fact. But I'm afraid that even you'll have to admit to failing occasionally.'

His slow, slightly cruel smile made her shiver slightly. It held a promise, almost a threat, of future retribution for that dig. 'What makes you think that I've given up where you're concerned?'

'Am I supposed to be grateful if you decide to take an interest in me again? Am I to let bygones be bygones, become a loving wife again and offer to share my bed and board with you?'

'I don't need a wife at the moment,' he said calmly.

'As to your other offer——' His voice held a musing note, as if he was weighing up the idea. 'I'll take a rain check on it, as our American friends say.'

'Really? Don't you mean that I'll have to take my place in the queue?'

'If you like,' he said. 'You may find that it takes more patience than you're capable of.' He turned to go.

'Or I may just decide not to bother,' she told him. 'You're not the only fish in the sea, you know.'

He smiled with genuine amusement this time. 'And neither, my dear wife, are you. Don't forget that, will you?' And on that note he left her.

As the days went by, it seemed that he had every intention of drawing her attention to the fact as he was seen all over the town with the perfectly-groomed Michèle Durand draped on his arm or smiling fondly at him from the passenger seat of the gleaming black Porsche that was still apparently his favoured choice of car. Its sleek, gleaming lines somehow reminded Cassie of its owner, elegant yet powerful, in a class of its own and capable of easily outdistancing its nearest rivals. It was an attraction that Michèle obviously felt too.

Cassie almost bumped into them one morning as she was making her way along the Rue de la République with a heavy bag of Saturday shopping, heading for home and the long, cool drink that she felt she had earned after her tussles with the varying shopkeepers. They were hogging the narrow pavement, engrossed in conversation, and they didn't get out of her way until it was almost too late to avoid them. Then Elliott had put a possessive arm around Michèle's waist and he had moved her gently out of Cassie's way as if she had been a valuable piece of china about to be mown down by her heavy, clumsy approach.

Looking at the older woman's casual smartness Cassie felt even more like an ungainly hobbledehoy in her oldest jeans and a tee-shirt that had definitely seen better days. She had no make-up on and her hair was tied in a loose knot on top of her head in an effort to keep cool. She saw Elliott glance from one to the other of them and assumed that he was making the obvious comparisons. Michèle looked fashionable enough to grace any man with her company, while she herself looked just plain scruffy.

A frown marred Michèle's perfect features at the interruption. '*Imbécile!* Can't you look where you're going?' she demanded in her own language. 'You nearly knocked me over!'

'Miss Russell invariably acts before she thinks,' Elliott offered by way of explanation. 'But there's no harm done.'

'Miss Russell?' Michèle's interest was aroused. 'You know this person, Elliott?' She sounded as if she could not believe that he mixed with such rabble.

'You could say that.' His eyes raked over Cassie's flushed face. 'You haven't been formally introduced, have you? Michèle, this is Cassandra Russell from my office. This is Madame Durand, Cassandra. You may have seen her with me at the Belle Madeleine a few evenings ago.'

'This, *this* is the girl at the restaurant the other night?' Michèle asked wonderingly, making it unflatteringly plain that she had not recognised Cassie in her everyday clothes. Or maybe she had just decided to blot her from her memory as unworthy of note, Cassie decided. '*C'est possible?*'

They shook hands reluctantly. His wife and his mistress, Cassie thought in a sudden fit of mild hysteria. Only Elliott would dare to bring the two of them together and expect them to be polite to each other in his presence. But Michèle did not know of Cassie's claim upon her escort and could afford to be gracious and greet her with an appearance of courtesy. She gave Cassie a cold, slightly condescending smile, as if saying, 'Look what I've got. Don't you wish he was yours?'

'Miss Russell, I am charmed to see you.' She had a low, husky voice that men would find extremely sexy and she knew it and capitalised on the fact, Cassie was sure.

Liar, she thought, as she smiled stiffly in return. 'I've just been doing some shopping,' she explained unnecessarily. 'I was hurrying home.'

'Ah, yes,' said Michèle with the bored air of one who always had those things done for her. She turned and put a small, possessive hand on Elliott's arm. 'Then we will not keep you. *Chéri?* Shall we go? The table is booked for lunch and we are already late.'

'We wouldn't have been, if it hadn't taken you so long to get dressed,' he told her lazily.

The meaning was clear to Cassie's mind, the implied intimacy of the remark strangely hurtful. Did an ex-wife always have this dog-in-a-manger feeling about the man to whom she had been married? Did it wear off in time or would she still be jealous of Elliott's choice of mate as the years went by? She hoped that there would be enough distance between them in future for him not to be able to flaunt his women in front of her in this insulting way.

He was smiling down at Michèle now and Cassie, watching them as if incapable of turning away, thought how compelling his charm could be when he chose to use it. Not that he had wasted much in her direction recently. But she was only the wife of whom he had tired and neglected to discard.

'Of course. Let's go.' He nodded pleasantly, dismissively, to Cassie and they were gone, swallowed up in the crowds.

Elliott had said that no woman had ever succeeded

in pushing him around, but Michèle seemed pretty well in command, Cassie brooded as she unpacked her groceries back in her rooms. She slammed down a bag of onions viciously, wishing that she could have thrown them at the other woman's elegantly coiffured head.

Well, she was welcome to him. And, if that was the sort of woman he wanted, then he could have her and she wished him any happiness that he found with her. The days when she herself had laid claim to his love were, after all, long since over. She wondered if he would ask Michèle to marry him. Had he told her that he had been married before? Perhaps they had been too busy with other things to get round to discussing it yet.

Would he approach her himself when he decided that he wanted a divorce or would the communication be an impersonal one through his London solicitors? Perhaps he was waiting for her to make the first move? Cassie frowned at the thought. Did she want to do that? She had been content to let matters drift for the last five years, exactly why, she did not know. She supposed she had been following the maxim of letting sleeping dogs lie. She had not wanted to precipitate a meeting with her husband until she had felt completely able to cope with him. But if she had not gained enough confidence after all this time away from him, it seemed scarcely likely that she would acquire it now. She was all too well aware of her woeful inadequacies in that direction.

She supposed she should really be grateful to Michèle. If the woman managed to get Elliott to the point of offering marriage, it would at least give Cassie her freedom. And she would make better use of it this time, she decided. She was not an impulsive girl any longer, determined to grab everything that she wanted from the world in the instant that she saw and desired it. That was the sort of mad action that had brought Elliott into her life in the first place. *And* the ensuing heartbreak.

Yet the traitorous thought that, if she had her time again, she would have done exactly the same crept unbidden into her brain. Only she would not have made the mistake of walking out on Elliott and leaving the field clear for a succession of other women to take over from her.

Why was it that Elliott still held the same virile attraction for her that had first swept her off her feet? For night after night she had lain sleeplessly in bed analysing her reactions to him that night in the garden of the Belle Madeleine. Perhaps physical feelings still remained long after all other stimuli in the marriage had gone. What other way could she explain the fact that her body responded to Elliott's touch in the same manner that it had always done even though her mind resisted him?

But that was no excuse. To admit that she was ruled by physical passion was accepting that she was little better than the slut that he had accused her of being. Next time she got involved with a man she would choose friendship and tenderness, not the sort of conflict and passion that her relationship with Elliott had produced. And she would be happier for it, she told herself.

Standing in the middle of the bright kitchen with her shopping half unpacked, she suddenly paused as the truth hit her. There couldn't be a next time until she had disentangled herself from the stranglehold that Elliott had upon her. And she didn't want to free herself from him, for all her protestations to the contrary.

It was then that she admitted the truth to herself. She still loved Elliott Grant.

CHAPTER SEVEN

WHEN Cassie went into the office the following Monday, she was sure that the realisation that had dawned on her so dramatically must be written all over her face. But it seemed that Jules noticed no startling change in her, since he merely asked her casually if she had had a good weekend.

'Fine, thanks,' she responded automatically as she sat down at her desk.

'I rang your landlady's number on Sunday morning to see if you felt like coming out for the day, but she said that you weren't there.' He sounded faintly accusing.

She had not been out with him since that one disastrous outing, dodging his invitations tactfully and hoping that she was not making her refusals too pointed. Somehow, she had not felt like going anywhere in Jules' company. Until now she had not been able to think why that could be, but with the knowledge that she was still in love with Elliott, she realised the reason only too clearly. Jules was a pleasant, even entertaining man, but he would never be anything more than a friend. Pleasant and entertaining were the last words that anyone could apply to Elliott's behaviour towards her, but it did not matter. She loved him whatever he was and whatever he did, and if Jules tried for a thousand years, he could never fill her with the same emotion for him.

She smiled rather forcedly at her colleague. 'I'm sorry. It was such a glorious day that I thought I'd go for a walk.'

She had sought refuge in the still quietness of the Alyscamps, a poplar-lined avenue where rested the stone sarcophagi of ancient times. Usually it was a favourite tourist haunt and they flocked along the pathway leading to the small, ruined church of St Honorat eagerly photographing the picturesque sight that the scene made. But Cassie had got there early and, apart from a solitary artist, totally absorbed in sketching the view that had attracted many painters in the past, among them Van Gogh and Gauguin, there was no one to disturb her thoughts as she had walked along, for once unaware of the sombre beauty of the place.

How did you come to terms with the discovery that, after a bitter parting and five years away from the man, you were still as hopelessly bowled over by him as ever you had been? And, having admitted the truth to yourself at last, what were you to do about it? Cassie had perched on the cold stone of a block of fallen masonry and tried desperately to think of a solution to the problem. It was like one of those ghastly exercises that appeared in schoolgirls' textbooks. Cassandra is in love with Elliott. But Elliott is attracted to Michèle. Cassandra and Michèle both want Elliott. Which girl does he choose and why?

She had smiled ruefully at that. Putting herself and Michèle side by side as they had been in the street yesterday and asking Elliott to choose between them was like demanding that he judge a beauty contest between Beauty and the Beast. Oh, Cassie knew that men had considered her attractive and that Elliott himself had been fairly impressed by her when he first met her, but there was no way that she could compete with the glamour and sophistication of Michèle Durand.

Cassie was frank and straightforward and likely to say the first thing that came into her head, impulsive to the end. Michèle was the type who thought and

thought again before she launched into speech, a calculating woman who never muddled her emotions with
her guiding sense of logic. All they had in common
was their feeling for Elliott, and even in that they
differed. Cassie wanted the man that she loved and
Michèle the man that she had decided would be the
most suitable husband for her. Cassie knew perfectly
well that if Elliott had been a poor man the Frenchwoman would, possibly with regret, have not allowed
herself to go all out to attract him.

Of course it was idiotic to see the matter in terms of
a straight fight between herself and Michèle with the
dice loaded in the other woman's favour because of her
greater assets in the battle. That was to ignore the views
of Elliott himself, to regard him simply as a pawn in
the game. And by no stretch of the imagination could
he be called that. He might decide that Michèle, like
Cassie, lacked the necessary qualities that he demanded
in his ideal woman. She scarcely supposed he would
have much compunction in ditching her in that case
and finding, with equal ease, a succession of attractive
women with whom to while away his time until he hit
upon the one that he did want to make the second Mrs
Grant.

Whatever Elliot decided to do, it was evident to
Cassie that she had not a cat in hell's chance of winning
back his love. From their first meeting here in France
he had been coldly detached and far from the passionate lover that she had once known. Even when he had
kissed her he had been totally in control of himself. It
had not bothered him that, in visiting the Arles office,
he would come face to face with his wife, because he did
not care about her one way or another any more. If he
thought about her at all, she supposed, it was as someone in his past who had caused him more irritation
than he normally expected from his women.

And he seemed to despise her for that. When she had implied that she had found no difficulty in replacing him in her affections it had seemed no more than he had expected somehow. As if she was the sort of woman who kept no moral standards. And that had hurt her, especially, coming as it did from a man whom she had caught almost in the act of infidelity. Was Elliott really old-fashioned enough to hold to a code of morals that allowed total freedom to the male and expected the female to accept such behaviour as normal? That was completely archaic! Surely no woman would stand for that kind of treatment in these liberated days?

She had sat for two hours until the discomfort of her perch had forced her to her feet again and she had found herself surrounded by an influx of tourists, recently disgorged from the brightly-painted tour bus at the entrance to the Alyscamps. She was not likely to get any more peace there, she realised, with the prospect of more coaches to follow this one, and she fled homeward, even less sure of what she should do than when she had begun to ponder the question.

'Cassie! For the third time of asking——' Jules' voice broke in on her reflections.

'Sorry.' She turned a startled face in his direction. 'What's the matter?'

'I think that's what I should be asking you. You seemed to be in a little world of your own.'

'I have got things on my mind at the moment,' she admitted guiltily. If only Jules knew what the problem was!

'Anything that I can help you with?' He sounded intrigued.

'No, it's nothing really. Only the taxing question of whether to buy a dress that I saw on Saturday,' she lied glibly. 'A weighty decision that only another woman would understand.'

'But we Frenchmen are well skilled in our judgment of such matters and able to please our womenfolk by advising them. We are not like your cold English husbands and lovers who regard such things as effeminate. See, I have the perfect solution for you instantly. Buy the dress and then wear it to come out with me next weekend, seeing that you were not able to manage it last Sunday.'

She laughed. 'We'll see.'

'Promises, always promises, Cassie. Do you never commit yourself to anything?'

'Never,' she told him firmly. 'It's part of my charm.'

He pulled a rueful face. '*Vraiment*. And it works for you. But how many men have you driven to distraction by your behaviour?'

'Quite a few, I should imagine,' came Elliott's sardonic voice from behind them. 'For some English girls, playing the tease with their boy-friends is as popular a sport as the bullfights that you enjoy so much in this part of the world. It's a just comparison really. In both the object is to see how far you can bait the victim and still avoid injury yourself.'

'But we do not kill the bull here in Provence,' said Jules, slightly puzzled by the obvious bitterness in the other man's tone. 'Only in Spain does he bite the dust.'

'And sometimes,' said Cassie, entering the argument with spirit, 'the bull gets the better of his opponent.'

'If he's unusually tough and quick on his feet,' Elliott countered.

'Some bulls are.'

He gave a faint nod of acknowledgement. 'I'm glad that you're aware of the fact, Miss Russell. It never pays to judge animals or people as if they're all alike. Sometimes the individual may surprise you by his actions, if you're not expecting them.'

'It's not a mistake that I usually make,' she said.

'No?' One dark brow challenged the statement.

'I have every confidence in my ability to spot the rogue in every herd,' she told him smartly. 'And they *are* the dangerous ones, aren't they?'

'And are you equally confident of your power to deal with them when you've separated them from the common run?'

'Naturally.' She raised her head, meeting the speculative look in his dark eyes defiantly.

Jules broke the tension with a laugh that reminded them of his presence. 'What is all this talk of animals? I feel as if I am in a zoo, not an estate agent's office,' he added, giving an expressive lift of his shoulders. 'This is ridiculous.'

Elliott threw Cassie a mocking smile that told her more clearly than words could have done exactly what he thought of his supposed replacement in her life. 'It appears that we have left Monsieur Pinot somewhat behind.'

'Oh, he keeps up with me very well in other things,' Cassie replied sweetly. Let him make what he liked of that remark!

A quick flame of anger kindled in his eyes and she knew that the intended gibe in her answer had gone home. 'Indeed?'

'I have just been trying to persuade Cassie to come out with me this weekend and allow me to demonstrate to her how well we could get on.' After Elliott's apparent willingness to talk something other than business with his staff in the middle of a Monday morning, Jules felt emboldened to speak to him half jokingly, man-to-man.

Elliott gave a thin smile and Cassie wondered if he was about to deliver one of his sudden freezing setdowns. 'And the lady's reluctant to oblige you? What can she be thinking of?'

'It would never do to give in on first time of asking,' she said hastily. 'Surely you know that, Mr Grant?'

'Then you'll come?' Jules asked eagerly.

She smiled full at him, totally excluding Elliott from the gesture. 'Of course. I'd love to.'

She sensed Elliott's displeasure as he told them, 'Well, if that's settled, perhaps we can get back to running a business.'

There was an edge to his voice, but Jules, a less acute listener, missed it and laughed as he voiced cheerful agreement and bent his head to his work again. After Elliott went out he raised his head and said, surprised, 'He was quite human for once. I wonder what brought that on?'

'I wonder,' said Cassie, and silently cursed her husband. Thanks to her desire to spite him she had accepted an invitation that she would otherwise have refused. And in doing so, paradoxically, she had put herself even further in Elliott's black books. Perhaps she would be able to find a way out of seeing Jules without upsetting him too much. She took no pleasure in the prospect of hours spent in the company of a man who would never inflame her mentally or physically however hard he tried. And it was not fair to let him make the effort.

But, try as she might, there seemed no way, short of inventing a dying relative at the opposite ends of the earth, that she could get out of the planned excursion that Jules had fixed for the following Saturday. As the week went by with alarming rapidity, Cassie realised with resignation that she would have to go through with it all.

'You like the sea, do you not, *ma belle*?' Jules asked. 'We'll set off early and go to the coast, to La Grande Motte. We can swim and laze about the beach if it's a nice day.'

'Yes, that sounds good,' she said. At least he could hardly make a heavy pass at her on the public beach with other people about. She shut her mind to what possibilities he might make of the drive to and from the coast with the return trip late in the evening if Jules ran true to form.

The faint hope that it might pour with rain was dispelled on Saturday morning when she padded to the window in her nightdress and peered resignedly out at the prospect of a really sunny, cloudless day. The blue sky and glowing yellow of the sun mocked her.

'Damn you, Elliott Grant, for getting me into this,' she muttered as she showered, put on her bikini and reached for her new pale green sundress to wear over it. She found her towel and sun lotion and rooted out a broad-brimmed sunhat just in case the heat became too much for her. Then, after a quick breakfast, she ran downstairs in response to the impatient hooting of a car horn outside the house. Jules had impressed upon her the need for an early start to beat the holiday crowds and he had certainly arrived on the dot. It was only just on half-past eight.

Cassie closed the door behind her and looked for Jules' small sports car, frowning when she did not spot it immediately. Had she been mistaken, after all?

'The car's parked down the road. There wasn't enough space up here.' Elliott's voice sounded behind her and she whirled quickly around to confront him.

'You! Where's Jules?'

'He sends his apologies,' he told her smoothly.

'And a lot of use they are. Where is he?'

'It really wasn't his fault. I needed him to go to Marseilles with some clients who arrived unexpectedly very late last night and who phoned me at home very early this morning. They're on a flying visit to do business and today was the only time they could spare to look at properties in the area.'

'Why couldn't you have taken them yourself?' she asked suspiciously. 'If they're such great buddies of yours that they have no qualms about disrupting your beauty sleep I'd have thought you would have been only too eager to deal with them personally.'

'I'm not as familiar with the roads round there as Pinot is. Besides, it's only by doing the job that he'll learn it.'

'To the extent of giving up his free time?'

'It's sometimes necessary to make sacrifices in order to get ahead,' he told her.

'Oh, of course. You'd know all about that, wouldn't you, Elliott?' she said. She was half relieved to be reprieved from the day ahead and half angry with Elliott for daring to interfere with her arrangements. She shrugged. 'Oh, well, thank you for telling me the expedition's off.' She turned to go inside again.

His hand on her arm halted her as she took a step away from him. 'Who says it's off? I've come to offer myself as a substitute for Pinot.'

She looked at him, aware of the strong appeal that he made to her senses this morning. He had discarded the formal business suit that he habitually wore at the office in favour of more casual dress: a tee-shirt, unbuttoned at the neck to show the tanned column of his throat and reveal a glimpse of dark, hair-roughened chest, and a pair of faded jeans that hugged his lithe, flat-stomached figure. On his bare feet were a pair of espadrilles. He looked dangerously attractive, she thought. And dangerous was the operative word.

His voice held that note of persuasion that she had never been able to resist. 'It's a beautiful day, too good to waste sitting at home on your own. We can still go to the beach, Cassandra. And I've brought a picnic for us in the back of the car.'

She looked at him warily. 'You managed to get a picnic together after your clients rang you and you fixed it all up with Jules? They must really have rung you at the crack of dawn.'

'They did,' he said calmly.

She hesitated and was lost.

'Come on, Cassandra. What's the good of cutting off your nose to spite your face? You want to come, don't you?'

She did, but not for the reasons he imagined. He thought she was trying to conquer her dislike of him in order to enjoy the trip ahead. He little knew that the only thing stopping her from gladly agreeing to go with him was the fear that she would do something to reveal how very far from hating him she was. And that would never do.

'I'm surprised that you're so eager to escort me,' she fenced. 'You haven't seemed too eager to spend time in my company.'

'Circumstances alter cases.' He smiled at her, a warm, irresistible smile that softened the arrogant hardness of his face. 'Well?'

It occurred to her to ask what the circumstances were that so changed his contempt of her into an apparent sudden desire for her company. But she dismissed the thought. Why analyse Elliott's motives? Why not just live for the moment and the prospect of a whole day of further delightful moments with him in this good mood? She capitulated. 'Well, if you're my only hope of a day by the sea——'

'Good.' He sounded pleased. He led her to the car and opened the door for her, making sure that it was shut firmly behind her after she had got in.

A curious fancy made her liken the action to banging

the cell door on a prisoner. 'Making sure that I don't
have second thoughts and try to escape your clutches?'
she asked him half seriously, as he settled into the
driver's seat.

He did not ask her what she meant. That was one
virtue of Elliott's: he never misunderstood a reference
she made or failed to pick up a point that she made.
'What do you think?' he mocked her, and she felt a
sudden moment of unease.

She could suppose that he was eager to have her company. 'What would you have done if I decided not to
come with you?'

'Are you imagining that I might have slung you over
my shoulder and carried you off in approved fashion?'
His eyes glinted wickedly. 'I'm sorry to disappoint you,
Cassandra, but I don't usually need to employ such
tactics and I'm hardly likely to make an exception in
your case.'

'So what would you have done?' she persisted.

He shrugged. 'No point in wasting the picnic. I expect I might have found someone else who was willing
to share it.'

Michèle, she presumed, although she could not see
the lady enjoying the experience. To her the beach
would mean the fashionable resorts east of Marseilles
where the jet set went to see and be seen. Yet, if Elliott
had invited her, no doubt she would have gone without a murmur. Suddenly a shadow came over the
brightness of the day. She did not ask him whether he
would have preferred another companion. He might
have said yes.

The powerful car ate up the miles to the coast. It
seemed that Elliott was in a determinedly good mood
this morning, treating her for once like a reasonable
human being instead of an errant wife who had offended beyond all forgiving. His manner was friendly,

but impersonal, almost as if he was entertaining a client, as he remarked on a group of black bulls with their attendant *gardien* astride his horse driving them along the road to a farm, or the distant sight of rare, pink flamingoes rising about a marshy, reed-fringed pool on the horizon.

She responded amicably. There was no point in stirring up controversy about anything. She knew how the smallest difference of opinion between them seemed to lead to a blazing row these days. And, with the whole day stretching tantalisingly ahead of them, she had no desire to provoke a resumption of his bad temper. It was best to follow his lead and assume an air of polite compliance, whether she felt it or not. In fact, it was an effort not to show the joy that she was feeling at being in his company.

She would have liked to have questioned him further about the mystery clients who had turned up and demanded attention, but she had the feeling that Elliott had said all that he intended to say about the day's rearrangements. What was the point of arguing anyway? she reasoned. Perhaps, just for one day, she could fool herself that they were still together, happy and loving and completely engrossed in each other. She leant back in her seat with a sudden sigh of pleasure.

He sensed the feeling, she was sure of it, and he relaxed slightly. They drove on in silence for a while, but it was a companionable one. By the time the futuristic apartment blocks, built in the shape of pyramids, came into view, Cassie had been lulled into a feeling of quiet content. She was with the man she loved. For one day she and not Michèle Durand would have his exclusive attention. And who knew what might come of it?

Elliott parked the car and they set off for the beach.

Cars were banned on the pedestrian walks of the town and it made a pleasant change.

'La Grande Motte was specially designed and developed as a holiday resort,' Cassie explained. 'They reckon that thousands of people come here every summer. And it's growing in popularity all the time, for the French themselves as well as with foreign visitors.'

Elliott scanned the vast expanse of golden beach that was mercifully comparatively uncrowded. 'I'm all for progress, but I'm glad we seem to have caught the place on a reasonably quiet day.'

'It's early yet,' she reminded him. 'Still, it is nearly the end of the season and the crowds are generally around at the height of the summer.'

'A swim first?' he suggested, and she nodded enthusiastically. How different the clear blue of the Mediterranean always was from the muddy grey waters back home! Although the temperature could be just as cold, she reminded herself.

They deposited their things on the sand and prepared for the water. Elliott was ready first and Cassie's heart missed a beat at the sight of his hard, muscled body, his all-over tan emphasised by the brief black trunks that he wore. He looked lean, fit and attractive. It was all that she could do not to close the distance between them and run her hands over the tall, virile length of him. She swallowed hard.

She undressed slowly, curiously reluctant to let him see her in the fashionable bikini that was little more than two strips of lacy material. It was silly, she knew, to be self-conscious, but she could not help herself. She fiddled with the buttons of her sun-dress and was suddenly aware of his gaze on her.

He knew what was bothering her and had no hesitation in broaching the subject with some amusement. 'Suddenly coy, Cassandra? There's really no need to

worry. I've seen all you have to offer before, if you remember.' And now it no longer excited him, was what
she inferred from his tone.

'I wasn't worrying,' she snapped back at him.

'My mistake. I was imagining that you thought that
you might have run to fat in the last five years out here
lotus-eating.'

'What do you think?' she challenged him. She undid
the last button, slid out of her dress long-limbed and
enviably slender and turned to him for his opinion.

He studied her for a long moment, his eyes lingering
on her shapely legs and going upwards to inspect every
line and curve, before coming to rest on her face.
There was a glint in his expression that Cassie suspected and suddenly, without waiting for an answer
from him, she raced past him to the sea. He caught her
up before she reached the waves, but did not try to stop
her as she was afraid that he might and they plunged
into the clear water together, Cassie shrieking at its
sudden cold against her sun-warmed skin.

They swam out a little distance, revelling in the feel
of the water once they had grown accustomed to its
first chill. This was a kind of heaven, Cassie reflected
as she floated dreamily, closing her eyes and letting the
sun beat down on her face, bathing it in warmth. A
sudden tug at her feet reminded her of Elliott's presence and she spluttered as she went under, gulping and
spluttering as she swallowed a mouthful of sea-water.
She struck out for her tormentor and he let himself be
caught with surprising ease. She realised why when his
arms wrapped themselves firmly round her and his
dark, water-sleekened head bent over hers, his mouth
claiming hers fiercely.

He tasted of salt water as his mouth pressed against
her. She trod water as she pressed herself nearer to
him, reluctant to break away, although she knew that it

was madness to allow him the liberty of treating her as if she was still his wife, always at hand to be fondled, if the mood took him.

She remembered their honeymoon in Bermuda when they had luxuriated like this in the clear turquoise waters near the private beach bungalow that a friend of her parents had generously made available to them for as long as they cared to use it. After a night of rapturous lovemaking they would go for a pre-breakfast swim which invariably ended with Elliott carrying her the hundred yards or so from the sea back to the bedroom. Sometimes they had not even got as far as the house. Breakfast had inevitably been eaten late in those idyllic days.

She forced herself to fight free of him, suspecting from the ease with which she managed her escape that he had not felt like preventing her. Did Elliott still think back to those honeymoon days when they had assumed that their love would last for ever and no shadow had fallen over their married life? It would be nice to believe that, just occasionally, he had happy memories of their time together instead of carrying away only bitter thoughts. She did not feel sufficiently sure of herself to ask him.

She swam for a little longer, then, feeling the chill despite the heat of the sun, she headed for the shore. Elliott joined her after she had towelled herself vigorously and donned the long-sleeved towelling beach-robe that she decided to bring along at the last minute. She felt better and more able to cope with Elliott's company without exposing her almost naked body to his interested gaze. He might not care for her as a wife any more, but as a woman she still held attraction for him— he had admitted as much after the episode at the Belle Madeleine. He might have Michèle to share his bed, but she was temporarily unavailable. Fidelity had never been his strong suit and he might just decide to enlarge upon the kiss that he had just stolen from her. And, if he attempted to do so, she reckoned little on her chances of stopping him.

It seemed, however, that his mind was on other, more basic requirements as he deposited his powerful body on the sand beside her, wiping away the droplets of water that still clung to his bronzed skin. 'Do you feel ready for lunch yet?'

She watched, as if hypnotised, the play of his muscles as he towelled himself dry with quick, sure movements. 'What?' she floundered, dragging her eyes to his face and realising from the look of sardonic amusement there that he had been quite aware of her preoccupation. 'Oh, yes, I'm ready for lunch. The sea air always gives me an appetite.'

'And is Jules always able to satisfy it?' he enquired with dangerous softness.

He wasn't talking about lunch and they both knew it. Did he think that she looked at Jules like that, with the same expression of naked longing on her face? Cassie supposed he did. As far as he was concerned she, like him, availed herself of the attentions of any member of the opposite sex who happened to be within range.

She deliberately misunderstood him. 'I've never been out for a picnic with Jules before. We've always eaten in a restaurant.' Which was true, she told herself, pacifying her guilty conscience at leading Elliott to believe that she and Jules were close companions. On the one and only occasion that he had taken her out, they had eaten at the Belle Madeleine.

'He must have money to burn,' Elliott commented. 'Perhaps we're over-paying him.' He reached out for the basket and began to unpack it. 'I'm afraid I can't

offer you anything exotic,' he said, taking out a long
loaf of French bread, a crock of butter and an earthen-
ware dish containing pâté, 'but you used to like this
sort of thing and I assumed that your tastes hadn't
changed.'

'They haven't,' she told him, deftly relieving him of
the red and white checked cloth on which the meal was
to be spread and anchoring it down on the sand.

'That's a relief. They seemed to have altered rather
drastically in other areas and not necessarily for the
better.'

'Meaning?' she asked, knowing full well that he was
referring to her apparent choice of male companions.
Just let him criticise Jules. She could think up enough
comments of her own about the beautiful Michèle.

He met her eyes mockingly and refused to give her
that satisfaction, although he knew what she was thinking, of that she was sure. 'Your hair,' he instanced.
'You never used to have it in that awful school-marm
style. It's a crime to scrape it back as if you were
ashamed of it.'

She had brushed it severely away from her face and
tied it up in a bunch on top of her head in a deliberate
effort not to arouse Jules' interest further by looking too
attractive. The soft waves of red, falling to her shoulders in wanton abandon, gave her a free, untamed look
which most men saw as a challenge. It attracted them
to her like bees to a honeypot and she had no intention
of encouraging Jules to behave in the same way.

But somehow she didn't care if it had that effect on
Elliott. If she admitted the truth to herself, she would
be glad if it did cast a spell over him. She reached up a
hand and pulled out the offending pins, shaking her
head and causing a red-gold cascade of hair to tumble
free. 'If I'd done that before I'd have looked like a

drowned rat after swimming,' she said. 'Better now?'
The excuse salved her pride at her instant compliance
with his wishes.

'Much better,' was all he said, but his gaze rested
over-long on her head, gleaming with liquid fire as the
sun caught it.

The swim had given them both a keen appreciation
of the food before them and they ate eagerly. The pâté
was followed by cooked chicken legs, accompanied by
crisp sticks of celery, firm red tomatoes and a bowl of
tangy cole-slaw mixture. Afterwards there was a mound
of fresh fruit and some sweet pastry confections made
with almonds.

Cassie stretched luxuriously and shook her head with
regret as Elliott offered her another apple. 'I couldn't
manage another thing, thanks. That was delicious.'

He took one himself and bit into it with evident enjoyment. 'I'm glad you liked it.'

Her eyes strayed to his lithe, flat-stomached body as
he moved, easing himself into a more comfortable position, and darted away again quickly as he caught the
look. She gave a sudden sigh. To any casual observer
they were a happy couple, lapping up the sunshine and
the sea air without a care in the world. Only they
were conscious of the atmosphere between them creating a wall of tension that was almost like a physical
barrier. Could anything that she did bring it tumbling
down? Was it even worth trying?

'What's the matter?' Alert as ever, Elliott heard her.

'Nothing.'

'That's no answer.'

He would have the truth if he cross-questioned her
all afternoon. She knew him well enough to realise
that. 'I was just thinking about our marriage.'

His voice sounded suddenly harsh. 'I wasn't aware
that we had a marriage any more.'

'No, I suppose we haven't.'

'Isn't it a bit late to be having regrets?'

'It's always a pity when something good between two people comes to an end,' she said quietly.

'And our marriage was something good?'

'I thought so once.'

He laughed, a bitter, mocking sound that jarred on her ears. 'Isn't it just like a woman to deliberately ruin her life past altering and then wish that everything was exactly the way that she had it before? It's no use, Cassandra. You can't recapture the past. You should have made more of it at the time. But now it's gone and best forgotten.'

What a naïve fool he must think her, moping over the ashes of a dead marriage. He had made it clear that he took no backward glances at the happier times. Could the break-up really have left him so unmoved, so happy to dismiss it and put it behind him as something in the dim and distant past of which he was no longer an interested observer?

She supposed it could, and cursed herself for the dull ache inside her which told her that she was completely incapable of doing the same.

CHAPTER EIGHT

SHE turned away from him, not wanting to continue the argument because it would be pointless to do so. They would only say things on either side that they would later regret. She would get over Elliott some day, she vowed. In the meantime she would just have to make the best of things. If this was the last day that she was ever to spend exclusively in his company—and she intended that it should be—she would not mar it with endless recriminations.

He seemed to be thinking along the same lines as he put his hands behind his head and lay back, enjoying the sunshine. 'Aren't you boiled alive in that?' His gaze rested on her wrap. 'Why don't you take it off? Or does modesty forbid?'

Cassie clutched it defensively to her and then forced her hands away. She was being silly. 'I will in a minute,' she said, rooting in her bag for her sunglasses. She waited until his eyes closed before stripping off the offending garment and lying down beside him. He said nothing, but she saw the corners of his mouth lift slightly in amusement. She banged her sunglasses on her nose and studied the sky through their smoked lenses. Damn Elliott! Why did he always see far more than any other man? She turned over and buried her face in her hands. She would try to ignore him.

They lay in peaceful silence for a few moments before his voice reached her again. 'Cassandra?'

'Yes?' Deliberately she made her tone drowsy as if she wanted to be left to sleep.

'Have you put any sunscreen on?'

She hadn't, although she had brought it with her. Her pale skin never soaked up the sun and she had always to be careful about exposing herself to its rays. 'No,' she said shortly.

'Then you better had,' he ordered her. 'You'll only burn if you don't.'

She knew that. But the demon within her bridled at his high-handed tone to her. 'I think that's up to me. You're not my keeper any more, Elliott, so stop treating me like an irresponsible four-year-old!'

He did not answer immediately and she thought that had settled the matter. But Elliott never gave in, she should have remembered that, and it was only when she felt a movement by her side and something cold and sticky in the the small of her back that she realised what was happening.

'What the——' She jerked up in an effort to find out what he was doing.

A firm hand pinned her to the ground despite her struggles and her husband's voice answered her with infuriating calm. 'If you will act like an irresponsible four-year-old you can hardly blame people for treating you as such. Now, lie still and let me put this stuff on your back for you before you start feeling the heat beginning to burn you.'

'I'll do no such thing!' she blazed at him, very much at a disadvantage because of his superior strength, but still prepared to go on fighting. 'Will you please let me go?'

'In a word, no,' he answered. 'What are you going to do about it?'

There was nothing that she could do and she soon accepted the fact as she writhed impotently for a few seconds under his grasp. 'Oh, go ahead, if it makes you happy,' she flung at him in the end, and lay unresisting, hoping that he would get it over with as quickly as possible. How dared he humiliate her like this!

But it appeared that Elliott was in no hurry. He unhooked her bikini top, leaving her back bare, and his hands lingered tantalisingly as he smoothed the lotion over her shoulders in leisured, rhythmic movements. His touch was like a trail of fire across her naked flesh. It was all that she could do to lie there and not respond to the invitation in the long, lean fingers as they moved slowly down her back towards the base of her spine. She tensed and shifted slightly. He was doing strange things to her pulse rate and he knew it. He was playing on her senses with deliberate provocation. She wanted to get to her feet, hold out her hand for the bottle and tell him that she could manage the rest for herself now.

But something stopped her, rooted her to the spot. His hands were travelling the length of her legs now, caressing and stroking as they moved upwards slowly until they rested lightly on the backs of her thighs, dwelling on their tapering softness and arousing her almost to fever pitch as the excitement within her mounted uncontrollably.

'All right?' he asked her softly.

He knew what he was doing to her and he was revelling in it, she thought. She supposed that he was demonstrating that he could exert a power over her if he cared to make the attempt. And he was succeeding admirably. Her limbs ached with the strain of forcing herself to lie cold and unresponsive as a log while all the time her body wanted nothing more than to surrender to him. It was a hard struggle and she was not at all sure that she was winning. She managed a stifled, 'Yes' in answer to him. She could not have said more to save her life.

'Turn over,' he told her, and there was no way that she could resist that dark note of command in his voice. She did not even think of suggesting that he should stop now and she knew that she was lost. He coated her legs with the lotion and they moved involuntarily under the pressure of his hands, on fire at his sure, expert touch. His expression was enigmatic as he moved forward over her stomach, his long fingers reaching upwards. She was glad that the dark glasses she wore hid the expression of wanton desire that must be in her eyes. Her whole body was alive and stirring at his touch. He was torturing her with his deliberate arousal of her feelings.

She could take no more. Her pride was conquered, lying here in the sand. She did not care what he thought of her. All that mattered was that he should take her in his arms and bring her the speedy relief that her senses cried out for. She raised her hands to grasp his forearms and, when he made no move to stop her, she ran her fingers lightly upwards, caressing the tanned skin of his upper arms and delighting in the smooth broadness of his shoulders.

'Elliott?' It was an entreaty to him. 'Please love me,' she pleaded.

He bent over her and removed the dark glasses from her face. For a long moment he studied her, then, apparently satisfied with what he saw, he lowered his body down against hers, his lips claiming her mouth in a deep, lingering kiss that lasted for an age, but seemed desperately brief as he left her to blaze a molten trail down her throat. He was as hungry for her, it seemed, as she was for him, responding with equal desire to her as she gloried in the feel of his near-naked body against hers, the thrust of his powerful thighs and the rhythmic beat of his heart against her chest. She folded her arms around him, pulling him closer to her, lost to the world in her need of him. She was aware of his hands removing the thin barrier that her flimsy bikini top made between them and then his lips were roving over her breasts, teasing and caressing her to a peak of almost unbearable pleasure.

Whether he intended to take her, here on the beach, she did not know. She was certain only that she would let him and feel no shame in the act. She was in a world of her own, far removed from the ordinary plane, aware of nothing and nobody except the man who had sent her to this higher level of consciousness. When he rolled suddenly away from her, his breath coming in short, ragged bursts, she was conscious only of an intense disappointment that the ultimate fulfilment was to be denied to her.

He stared at her, his eyes still dark with the smouldering desire that she had aroused in him. 'God help me, Cassandra, do you know what you're capable of doing to a man?' He thrust the bottle of lotion into her nerveless hands. 'Here, you'd better finish the job yourself, if you don't want me to do something that we might both regret.'

He turned from her abruptly, got up and ran from her towards the sea. Starting to her feet, she saw him wade in and swim strongly away from the shore. She could tell what kind of emotion was driving him from the force with which he was cutting through the water.

A low, appreciative whistle from a passing youth made her blushingly aware that the top part of her bikini lay on the sand at her feet and she crouched down instantly to pick it up and put it on. She knew that there were beaches in the South of France where nowadays almost anything went, but she was not the sort of girl for such public displays of her charms, however good her figure. She coloured at the thought of anyone watching herself and Elliott a few seconds ago. What could she have been dreaming of to let herself get so carried away?

She knew perfectly well, and that was the problem.

She loved Elliott now even more than she had done when she married him. Then she had offered him the affection of a naïve girl who knew little of the world and was content to see it through his eyes. Now what she felt for him was the love of a mature woman who has recognised her mate and asks nothing better than to join her forces to his for all time.

And Elliott? He was still an unknown quantity. Had he loved her five years ago, or did he feel morally obliged to put a ring on her finger before he took her virginity? Could their marriage have survived if she had closed her eyes to his shortcomings? She didn't know. Her brain was teeming with unanswered questions, all of them depending for a solution on the dark figure whose head was now a small dot out from the shore. And she was as far from sitting down with him and talking rationally about how he felt about such matters as marriage, divorce, reconciliation and the like as she had ever been.

She realised that the bottle of sun lotion still lay at her side where it had fallen when Elliott had thrust it at her. Automatically she took the top off and began smoothing the lotion on to her skin which still bore the traces of his touch. Would any man arouse her senses the way that Elliott did? She doubted it somehow. She thought of him with Michèle, kissing that invitingly red mouth, caressing the golden brown of her skin and stroking the tangle of platinum hair, and she felt physically sick with jealousy. Did Michèle have the ability to arouse him the way that she herself had just done? She had no way of knowing.

She sat where she was, straining her eyes in an attempt to keep pace with his whereabouts in the vast expanse of blue water. Finally she saw the dark head turning for the shore, the strong arms showing no sign of tiring as they moved effortlessly through the water.

She rolled over and lay on her front. It might be cowardly, but she could not sit and watch as he waded through the shallow water and over the sand towards her. She had not the nerve to scan his face to judge his present mood. No doubt he would make his wishes known to her.

The radar that had always operated for her when Elliott was near warned her as he approached and sat down by her side. She could feel his eyes boring into the back of her neck, willing her to turn round, but she lay still. She heard him sigh impatiently and then there was a long silence, broken only by the faint sound of his steady breathing. She twisted her head slightly and blinked a cautious eye in his direction, only to discover that, to all intents and purposes, he was asleep, his chest rising and falling rhythmically with each breath.

She considered the situation. Was he really asleep or just faking? You could never be sure of anything with Elliott. Was he really able to make passionate love to a woman one moment and totally ignore her the next, so unmoved in her presence that he could fall asleep at her side?

Cassie's tired brain could not cope with such strangely complex behaviour. The heat of the sun was pleasantly warm on her back, now adequately protected, thanks to Elliott. Perhaps he *was* asleep. In the far distance she heard the shouts of a family playing some kind of beach game and wondered in a drowsy way if they were playing rounders as her cousins had played with her when they had all been children. Did the French know how to play rounders? Cassie slept.

When she awoke the first chill breezes of evening were playing around her and Elliott was shaking her gently. She looked up at him with sleep-drugged eyes, not sufficiently awake to be embarrassed by their first encounter since they had so nearly played out a love scene to its natural conclusion.

'What time is it?' she asked.

'Time we were making tracks for home. You've been asleep for over two hours.'

'I must have been tired.' Or emotionally shattered.

'Perhaps,' he said. 'It's that kind of day. Are you ready to go?'

'Yes. Just give me a minute to tidy myself and put my dress on.' He was already dressed, she noticed.

She brushed the sand off her shoulders and put the green sundress on again, hating the sticky feel of her skin after using the sunscreen. If she had done without that, she thought, she might have felt better in lots of ways. She would not feel as if someone had run over her in a ten-ton truck, for one thing. A possible case of sunburn was little enough compared with what Elliott had put her through this afternoon.

He had picked up the luncheon basket and his towel and was waiting for her with his usual, faintly impatient air. He had never liked waiting around for people, she remembered. 'Ready? Good,' he said as she nodded her assent, and strode ahead of her to the car.

Cassie would not have connected this cool, casually polite man with the Elliott who had been her passionate companion of a few hours ago. Did he have absolute control over his emotions, she wondered, or was he genuinely unaffected? She followed him, stumbling in the fine sand in her efforts to keep up with his long stride. When she caught him up, he had already stowed the basket in the back of the car and had opened the passenger door for her. Swiftly she got in.

The journey back to Arles was completed in record time and almost total silence. As the miles flashed by all Cassie could do was to repeat over and over in her mind, 'This was my last chance of getting him back and I've thrown it away. I've thrown it away.' She glanced across at his lean face, impassive in the half light of the rapidly advancing evening. There was nothing to be gleaned from it.

'I wonder how Jules got on with the clients?' she ventured, and could have cut her tongue out once the remark had been made.

But strangely, the mention of the Frenchman did not seem to bother him. 'I think they'll have kept him busy,' he said with a sort of cold satisfaction. 'I hope you weren't expecting to rendezvous with him tonight and compare notes about the day. I doubt if he'll be back much before midnight.'

'You sound very sure of that,' she commented. 'Almost as if you'd arranged it that way.'

'Perhaps I did.'

'Not really?' She turned towards him, startled.

'Do you really think I'm capable of such a thing?' He sounded surprised.

She was having flights of fancy. 'No, of course not. You'd never play such a dirty trick.'

'All's fair in love and war.'

'Yes, but you're not in love with me, are you?' She tried hard to keep the wistful note out of her voice and was almost sure that she had succeeded.

Elliott paused a brief second before answering. 'No, Cassandra, I'm not in love with you,' he said deliberately.

She had wanted to know how he felt about her and now she did. So why did she feel as if the world was suddenly cold and empty and stretching barrenly before her? Did it matter that he had spelt it out to her at last? Of course it did.

Cassie stared blindly ahead, willing herself not to commit the final blunder and let the tears that were blurring her vision fall and disgrace her. She must keep herself from that folly at least. And it was because she was lost in such thoughts that she failed to notice which turning Elliott took after he had crossed the Rhône by way of Trinquetaille Bridge. It was only when he stopped the car in a completely alien quarter of town that she was jolted into a realisation that he had not, as she supposed, driven her straight home.

'Where are we?' she asked him.

'I am substituting for Jules today, am I not?' he said smoothly. 'I hardly think that he would have delivered you tamely back on your doorstep at this respectably early hour of the evening. He would have wined and dined you in style, I'm sure.'

'He would probably have consulted me as to what my wishes were in the matter first.'

'And you would surely have raised no objection.'

She met his challenging look and her gaze fell. If only she had known when she had embarked on this fiction of having Jules as her lover how difficult it would be to sustain, she would never have started it.

'Would you?' Elliott asked pleasantly.

'No.'

'Then you can hardly blame me for offering you the same service. I thought that you'd prefer an intimate dinner à deux to a crowded restaurant, so I've brought you back to the flat I've rented while I'm here. I'm sure Jules would have suggested something similar.'

And so was Cassie. But, while she would have had a fair chance of escaping unscathed from Jules' clutches, ladies' man though he was, she could hardly view an evening with Elliott in the same light. Elliott never took no for an answer when it was a matter of what he wanted. And if he wanted her as he had done this afternoon on the beach, she was lost.

Her mind ran in circles, trying to think of a valid excuse. A sudden headache, perhaps? But then her inner self took over, telling her that she would never learn how to handle a man like Elliott if she ran away from him all the time. It was the moment to be bold, to accept his invitation and to show him that she was capable of dealing with him. 'All right,' she said, surprising herself and him. 'I'd like to have dinner with you.'

He reached across her to open the car door for her, then led the way into the block of apartments outside which he had parked. Elliott's flat was on the second floor, a large, well-designed living and dining area, with a kitchen off it, and one bedroom with an adjacent bathroom. It was a perfectly organised bachelor flat. Decorated in shades of cream and brown, it looked cool yet inviting, and what furniture there was echoed the welcome: a scrubbed pine table, matching pine units in the small, but modern kitchen, deep, brown velvet chairs that looked squashy and comfortable and, at one end of the living room, an outsize, old-fashioned sofa, big enough to seat at least five people.

'It's nice here,' she said.

'I'm glad you like it.' He dumped the picnic things in the kitchen and waved a hand towards the bathroom. 'You'll remember that I don't like an audience when I'm cooking something. Why not take a shower when I'm getting everything ready? The water's hot and there are clean towels in the cupboard.'

'Thank you,' she said, a little uncertainly. 'I'd like that.' It was a pity that she had nothing to change into, but it couldn't be helped. The green dress was still comparatively fresh.

'And, Cassandra,' he called to her mockingly as she went in the direction that he had indicated, 'there isn't a bolt on the bathroom door, but don't worry that I shall bother you. I expect I'll be too busy cooking to be looking for a diversion.'

She heard him laugh as she went into the bathroom

and slammed the door loudly behind her.

The cares of the day seemed to drain away from her under the warm, reviving jets of water and, as she dressed again and brushed her hair vigorously, she felt ready for anything, when, determinedly cool and casual, she drifted back to the kitchen.

'Is there anything I can do to help?' she asked.

He didn't raise his head from the task of chopping herbs for the salad he had made. 'You can concoct some dressing for this, if you like. You'll find all you need in the cupboard above your head. I'll go and take my shower if you'll keep an eye on things here.'

'Right.' Cassie set quickly to work. It had been like old times to find Elliott in charge of the kitchen. He had always enjoyed taking over from her at the weekends, finding in the preparation of food a kind of therapy from the pressures of his everyday life. His tastes had run to fairly plain, English dishes, good, fresh food, simply cooked, as he called it. Tonight, it seemed, was no exception, and Cassie's mouth watered in anticipation as the appetising smell of steak wafted over to her.

He had laid the table and, when the food was ready, they carried it through and sat down to eat. Elliott opened a bottle of red wine and filled their glasses, raising his in a mock salute to her before he drank.

'To the future, Cassandra.'

'To the future,' she echoed dully, wondering how he could sound so cheerful. She glanced across the table at him and her heart somersaulted at his dark attraction. Freshly showered, with a tang of lemony cologne about him, and dressed in a black polo-necked sweater and matching tightly-fitting jeans, she would have defied any woman to remain unmoved by the picture that he made. And she was not any woman. She was his wife. But for how much longer?

After all that lay between them Cassie expected to find the conversation stilted and unnatural. But Elliott seemed determined to put her at her ease and talked easily and fluently about a number of topics, then skilfully drawing her out on the subject of her work here in France.

'You like it here, don't you?' he asked her curiously.

'Yes. I've been very happy here in Provence. The land and the people appeal to me enormously. It was a hard move to make, but I'm very glad I did.'

'How did your parents react to it?'

She shrugged. 'They worried—I suppose parents always do. But I think that after nearly five years out here I've proved that I can stand on my own feet now.'

He leaned forward to fill her glass again and she took a grateful sip of the wine. So far they had kept off painful reminders of the past. But how much longer could they avoid discussing the matters that some time must be raised between them?

'What about you, Elliott?' she asked, postponing the inevitable. 'You're now in the happy position of owning Prospect Properties and probably a lot else besides. How did you manage it so quickly?'

'Applied concentration and sheer hard slog,' he said, a slightly grim smile touching the corners of his mouth at the memory. 'When I put my mind to something I go all out to get it, and at that time it was a goal I had set myself.'

'And now you've achieved it, it doesn't matter as much?' she said softly.

'For me the challenge has always been in the attaining of the dream. The dream itself doesn't interest me too much. I've realised over the last——' he broke off and then continued deliberately, 'over the last four and a half years that there are other things in life besides business success, and I want to enjoy them before it's too late.'

'What sort of things?'

His intent gaze caught hers and held it. 'Love, marriage and possibly children.'

'To inherit the empire?' she taunted him.

He looked suddenly serious. 'If that's what they want. But I'll bring them up with a more balanced view of life and the importance of material success than I had. If they want to go off and become actors or artists or even dustmen, I won't stand in their way.'

'Dustmen earn a lot of money these days,' she said with a laugh. Then, seeing that he meant what he said, she went on, 'You've changed, Elliott. When I first knew you, nothing was allowed to stand in the way of your path to the top.'

'And human relationships were natural casualties. Yes, I know that now,' he said sombrely.

'So you're going to start again?' Off with the old and on with the new. But where did Michèle fit in with this vision of happy domesticity? Surely she wouldn't want children? They would ruin her figure and disturb her peace. Cassie couldn't imagine the sophisticated Frenchwoman dealing with the demands of chocolate-besmeared toddlers. Perhaps there would be a nanny.

'I have it in mind,' Elliott said calmly. He took their plates to the kitchen and returned with fresh fruit and cheese.

'Have you discussed it with the lady in question?' she asked him as he seated himself again. She could not bear to mention Michèle's name.

Her glass was half empty again and he topped it up before he replied. 'Not yet.'

'Do you—do you think that her ideas run along the same lines?' She put the question carefully.

'It may take a little persuasion on my part, but I have every hope of success.'

'I see.' There was nothing more to say. He seemed to be totally excluding her from his future life.

As if sensing her thoughts, he asked her abruptly, 'What about you? What are your plans?'

'I haven't any at the moment.'

'No? What about Jules and the others?'

'I think it would be better if we left Jules out of the conversation.'

'If you like,' he said, but she had the feeling that he would return to the topic. He was not easily deflected. 'Coffee?' he asked.

'Please.' Her head felt slightly heavy with all the wine that he had pressed upon her.

He made it while Cassie cleared the table and took the coffee pot and cups to a small, low table by the sofa. Its padded contours looked inviting, but Cassie hesitated as he sat down and patted the space beside him in silent command. But what was she worrying about? Elliott had made it clear that his plans for the future did not include her. She relaxed and sat down, taking the cup that he handed her.

'Black with a dash of cream and no sugar,' he said. 'Have I remembered correctly?'

She forced a smile. 'Yes. Very good.' She sipped the strong liquid and took a little consolation from its stimulating effect on her.

'Are you thinking of marrying Jules?' Elliott asked her suddenly, and she nearly choked on her coffee.

'He hasn't asked me,' she fenced.

He clicked impatient fingers. 'As if that mattered!'

She looked at him, wondering that he could not tell from the longing in her eyes that it was he, not Jules, that she wanted and always would. She managed to say coldly, 'What happens after I'm divorced from you is none of your affair.' Putting down her cup, she made a performance of looking at her watch and was genuinely shocked to find how the time had flown. 'I must go. It's long past my bedtime.'

He reached for her then, his arms sliding possessively round her as his lips nuzzled against her ear lobe. 'I agree,' he murmured. 'Long past time you were in bed.'

For an instant she made no response. Then she fought to get away.

His grip only tightened. 'What's wrong?'

'You know what's wrong. You're making love to me.'

'There's nothing wrong with that,' he told her lazily, studying her flushed face. 'We're married, remember? I can still claim my marital rights.'

'Then it's about time we had a divorce!'

'We'll talk about that later. Right now I've got other things on my mind.'

His mouth claimed hers and involuntarily her lips parted. She felt his hands on the buttons of her dress and the sudden freedom that indicated that he had slipped it from her shoulders. He pulled her down into the softness of the sofa and joined her there, covering her with his powerful frame. She could fight him no longer. She wanted him to make love to her as she had wanted it this afternoon on the beach. With a sigh she surrendered to him.

CHAPTER NINE

THE rays of the bright sun shining through the open
shutters directly on to her face woke Cassie next morning. For a moment or two she looked hazily around her
at the unfamiliar bedroom, noting the heavy, slightly
Victorian-looking wardrobe and its accompanying chest
of drawers and wondering how on earth she found
herself in such a place. Then, slowly, the memory of
what had happened last night came flooding back into
her brain and she smiled with contentment. She turned
to look for Elliott, but, although the pillow by her side
bore the imprint of his head, he was gone. She sighed
regretfully.

In a moment she would go and look for him, but at
present she was perfectly happy lying here thinking
about how happy he had made her. It was strange that
such a mixed bag of a day should have had such a
totally satisfactory ending. A reminiscent warmth stole
through her whole body at the memory of Elliott's
lovemaking. She stretched long and luxuriously and
then lay on her back, staring up at the ceiling with a
dreamy expression on her face. It had been wonderful.
Why had she allowed such a stupid thing as pride to
keep her away from her husband's side for so long?
Why had they wasted so many years apart? Of course,
she reasoned, it took two to make a quarrel and Elliott
could just as easily have made the first move. But it did
not matter any more.

Not after last night when he had picked her up from
the sofa in strong arms and had carried her tenderly to
the bedroom, depositing her on the large, old-fashioned

double bed. He had undressed her with tantalising slowness, his fingers straying and caressing her with lingering pleasure as he did so. His own clothes were discarded more swiftly and then he had come across to where she waited for him with eager, outstretched arms.

His kisses set her on fire with longing for him and he caught her up in a wild, spiralling rapture as his hands had roved over her possessively, bringing her sweet delight with every movement that they made. She had responded, showing him clearly what enjoyment he was giving her.

Yet, with a supreme effort, he had postponed the final act, she recalled. He wanted her, but even then he wanted her on his own terms. He wanted to hear the words that she had denied him for so long.

'Tell me you love me, Cassandra.'

'Oh yes, yes,' she groaned, lost in a world of pleasure and desire.

'Say it,' he insisted. 'I want you to say that you love me and no one else.'

'I love you,' she said obediently. 'No one else. I love you, Elliott.' And she had meant every word of the declaration that he had wrung from her.

His sensual, slightly cruel mouth had curved with something akin to satisfaction then and he had taken her fiercely with a rough, impassioned possession of her that had delighted her even as it scared her slightly with its force.

Her passion spent, she lay in his arms, her head resting happily against the hair-roughened skin of his chest. She could not bear him to move away from her and he seemed to feel the same, drawing her closer to him as if seeking a kind of reassurance that only she could provide for him. Long after he slept, she lay awake listening to the sound of his even breathing in the darkness and wondering what it was that drove him on, trampling down everyone who got in his way.

Was it really all an act? Underneath that tough, calculating exterior that he presented to the world, could he be as vulnerable as anyone else? Perhaps he could, although she knew that he would only ever reveal that side of him to those he loved or under extreme stress. She wondered into which category she came and a slightly bitter smile creased her mouth. She had certainly given Elliott a run for his money since she had come to Provence, even if she had capitulated at last. She pondered the point in a slightly dreamy way, not really concentrating.

'Cassandra?'

She moved against him, her lips wandering tenderly across his shoulder, leaving a trail of light, butterfly kisses there. 'Mm?' she asked him sleepily.

'Tell me again.'

'Why?' she said, kissing the hollow at the base of his strong, tanned throat.

'I like to hear you say it.'

She gave a low laugh of delight. 'I love you, Elliott Grant,' she said. 'Happy now?'

'Completely,' he answered her, and his mouth found her own again. This time his kisses were tenderly loving and he made her his with every effort to consider her pleasure as well as his. She had forgotten every wrong, real or imagined, that he had ever done her as she had gloried in the expertise of his lovemaking. She responded mindlessly to the feel of his firm mouth on hers and the heavy pressure of his body, pinning her down and keeping her a devoted captive, a slave obedient to his every wish.

Cassie stirred restlessly at the thought of the pleasure that they had shared. Surely after such a night he would not be able to tell her that he preferred another woman? Every muscle of his body had indicated his need of her and the joy that her response had given him. Whatever Michèle was like in that direction, Cassie somehow doubted if she could ever have pleased Elliott as she herself had done. Yes, she was very much afraid that Madame Durand was going to have a rude awakening when she discovered that a scruffy English girl had stolen her prize from under her very nose. Still, thought Cassie sleepily, I did have a few years' start on her.

She wondered what would happen now. She supposed it meant the end of the job at McIlroy and Wentworth. It would hardly do for the boss's wife to be working at a lowly post in the Arles office. She would have to take her place as Elliott's consort at the head of the empire in London. Cassie pulled a face at the prospect. She had tasted enough of the heady freedom of earning her own living to know that she could not bear to sacrifice her hard-won independence to become a mere cipher at her husband's side, smiling graciously at office functions and perhaps contenting herself with the usual run of coffee mornings in aid of charity. She had seen enough of that sort of business wife in her parents' set to know that it was not for her. What worse fate could there be for an intelligent woman than to have no real job to do in life?

Of course people of her mother's generation would argue that there was no more satisfying task in life than looking after a husband and their children when they came along. And it was true, perhaps. But Elliott had always shown an irritating tendency to be quite capable of looking after himself and, at present, there were no children to be considered. Still, after last night's little episode, that state of affairs might well be remedied in nine months' time. There might be a little girl with Elliott's large dark eyes and brown curls. Or a boy to inherit his ambition and stubborn sense of independence. It was to be hoped that the child, whatever sex it was, didn't have its mother's temper. Or its father's, for that matter!

The flat would be too small when they had children, she mused. They would have to look for a larger place, out in the country so that there would be fresh air and a garden for them to play in, but not so far from Town that Elliott had trouble commuting. She wanted to see something of her husband in future, not kiss him good-bye in the early morning and greet him late at night after the children were long since in bed. She laughed softly to herself. What a fool she was, going on like this! It wasn't even settled that she and Elliott would be living together again, although there could hardly be much doubt in the matter. They would have to discuss it all.

She must have fallen asleep again, for it was late when she jerked herself up to inspect the small ormolu clock by her side. Half the morning gone already, and she and Elliott had a good deal to talk over. Where was Elliott? She listened hard, but could hear no sign of anyone stirring in the apartment. What could he be doing? She supposed it was thoughtful of him to let her have a lie-in—after all she hadn't had much sleep during the night—but surely he would know that she wouldn't have minded if he had come and wakened her?

She sat up and looked round for her clothes. Her dress was still lying on the living room floor, she imagined. They had had other things to think about last night than worry about what she would wear today. And her beach robe was stuffed inside her towel some-where in the car where she had left it. She glanced around to see if Elliott had a dressing gown that she could borrow and drew a blank. But he always slept in the nude and had never bothered with such garments in their centrally-heated flat. It was hardly likely that he would bother here either.

Perhaps she shouldn't be worrying about it and she should just go in search of him as she was. After all, Elliott was her husband. He had seen her without clothes often enough for her not to be embarrassed about it. But she had always felt strangely self-conscious and much too inhibited to imitate his carelessness.

'Really, Cassandra, you are a little prude,' he had told her, when he had discovered her shyness and teased her about it. 'Do you think I don't know every line of your body, with or without your clothes on?'

'I wasn't thinking of you,' she had told him primly.

'Who, then?' His eyes mocked her wickedly. 'You're a married woman now. There's no need to worry about what Mummy will think about the way I've corrupted you!'

He never had liked her mother, blaming her for a lot of Cassandra's attitudes with which he didn't agree. 'Why don't you learn to think for yourself instead of throwing what your mother thinks at me all the time? I married you, not her,' he had told her during one of their ding-dong battles. Later she had seen his point of view and tended to agree with his criticism. But then Elliott hadn't been around to listen to her any more.

'I wasn't worried about my mother,' she said, teasing him. 'Just about the postman and the milkman and——'

He laughed. 'Well, if it stems from a reluctance to share your charms with anyone except your devoted husband, I'm all in favour.' And he bought her a frothy white negligee set, which had revealed as much as it concealed, to wear in the mornings.

'Completely impractical,' she told him severely.

'But you like it, don't you?'

'Yes,' she said. 'And I expect the milkman and the

postman will like it too.'

That had amused him and they had both laughed over it. Then they had been able to joke about infidelity, sure that neither of them would ever have cause to accuse the other of such things. Marriage break-ups happened to other people, never to them. Cassie smiled at the memory. In future they would never take anything for granted again. And certainly not their new-found happiness. They had been like a couple of children with their squabbling and fighting to gain points over each other. Now they had both matured and it would be better this time round.

'Elliott? Where are you?' she called, suddenly impatient to see him.

There was no answer and she sighed resignedly. Probably the heavy wooden door would muffle the last trump, if it sounded. She would have to go and look for him. Even if he'd gone out to collect milk or bread from the bakery that opened for the sale of freshly baked rolls even on a Sunday, she could make herself a cup of coffee and have one ready for him on his return. She pulled a sheet from the bed and, wrapping it round her toga-style with the ends hitched up so that she would not trip over them, she made her way to the door and opened it.

'Elliott?'

'In here,' his voice replied from the direction of the living room, and she ran eagerly forward to him.

'I'm ready for breakfast in bed, if you're still serving it. Even a cup of coffee wouldn't come amiss——' Her speech trailed away to a dismal halt as she rounded the corner and, looking for Elliott's tall figure, found that he was not alone. And the thunderstruck face of his companion belonged to Jules.

She stood dumbly looking at them. Then, realising that the sheet was not securely anchored around her as it might have been and was slipping over her shoulders, she grabbed frantically at it in a desperate attempt to arrest its descent.

'Cassandra!' Jules sounded horrified.

As well he might be, she supposed. It must be quite a shock to visit your employer's flat early on a Sunday morning and find your office colleague, the very girl that you'd had your own eye on and with whom you had seemed of late to be making some progress, fairly obviously involved with another man. In a state bordering on mild hysteria, all that she could think about was how much more shocked he would have been if she had stuck to her original thought and not bothered to wrap a sheet around her before coming in search of Elliott.

Cassie didn't know what she expected of Elliott. Hardly guilt or embarrassment: he was too much a man of the world to show either. Perhaps sympathy for her plight and an attempt to help her. But in that she was rudely awakened. When she tore her eyes from Jules' appalled face to study her husband, she surprised a look of mingled triumph and satisfaction there. A sudden suspicion took root in her mind. Elliott had engineered this scene with Jules quite deliberately. If she hadn't chosen that particular moment to wake up and make such an untimely entrance, he would have thought of some other way of ensuring that they met, she was sure of it. But why? What had he to gain from it?

He was completely in command of the stage, as always, looking carelessly attractive in figure-hugging slacks and a white tee-shirt, opened at the neck to display the tanned column of his throat. He had not yet found time to shave, she noticed absently, and the dark shadow round his jawline gave him a curiously piratical look. He was used to manipulating people and he was good at it. This little scene couldn't present too many problems to him, she thought bitterly, as she stood, rooted to the spot, and quite incapable of either fleeing or brazenly walking forward to greet them as if everything was perfectly normal.

'Sit down, Cassandra,' he commanded, and it did not occur to her to question the authority in his tone. She obeyed him, sinking gratefully into one of the comfortable brown armchairs. She did not think her legs would have held her up much longer.

Elliott blithely ignored her state of undress and its possible effect on Jules, treating her as if she had happened in on a perfectly normal business conversation to which she was entitled to contribute. 'Monsieur Pinot and I were just discussing his success with our clients yesterday,' he said in a pleasantly conversational tone. 'It seemed a tough assignment, but he appears to have coped with it admirably.' His dark eyes wandered over Cassie's figure, imperfectly concealed by the thin sheet, as he went on, 'He was rather worried about leaving you to your own devices at such short notice, just in the cause of business. I've been trying to reassure him. Perhaps you'll make a better job of it than I could. I did give you a good time, didn't I?'

There was no mistaking the implication in his voice. There was a silky satisfaction there and a sleek, smug look on his face, like a cat that had been at the cream. Cassie's hands ached to wipe it off with a hard slap that held all the force that she could muster. Jules loked as if he wouldn't mind setting about someone too, but whether it was herself or Elliott she couldn't decide. Perhaps he wasn't sure either.

Elliott crossed over to stand behind her chair and his hands came over its back to rest possessively on her bare shoulders. She tried to twist free, but his grip on her only tightened mercilessly and she was forced to submit to him. She would be a mass of bruises tomorrow from this rough treatment, she thought irrelevantly.

'Perhaps Cassandra is too shy to tell you how much she enjoyed the time that she spent with me yesterday,' he said softly, with deliberate provocation. 'But I can assure you that she showed her gratitude very prettily last night.'

'You bastard!' she breathed. How dared he shame her like this in front of Jules!

If he had hoped to incite the Frenchman to some kind of action, he was doomed to disappointment. Jules had evidently thought better of his impulse to punch somebody on the nose. Perhaps common sense had suggested to him that he would not get the better of Elliott if it came to a physical battle. He was the younger by several years, but Elliott was the fitter of the two men, as tough as steel and with a finely-honed strength that would bring him off the better in such an encounter.

'I see,' said Jules stiffly. 'Well, Cassandra is a free agent. She may do as she pleases.' For all his words there was a slight note of censure of her behaviour to be detected in his tone.

'Is that all you've got to say?' Elliott sounded faintly contemptuous.

Jules shrugged. 'What else is there to say?'

'Quite a lot!' With a sudden strength that she had not known she possessed, Cassie wrenched herself free of Elliott's hold and got to her feet. 'I'm not a parcel to be passed between you as if I had no will of my own.' She paused, wondering which was the best way to explain matters, and then decided that only the truth would serve. 'The fact is, Jules, that Elliott is my husband.'

'How brave of you to tell him. I wondered if you'd get round to it.' Elliott's mocking voice sounded behind her.

She ignored him. 'We've lived apart for several years, of course, and I've been using my maiden name at work. It was a little awkward when he turned up at the office. We decided it would be less embarrassing for all concerned if we kept quiet about the fact that we were married for the two months or so that he would be here in Provence.'

'You'd already put the memory of your marriage vows long behind you,' her husband interrupted her mockingly.

'And now,' she said coolly, trying to keep the hurt at Elliott's betrayal from her voice, 'it seems that the secret is out at last.' She was aware that in her brief statement she had glossed over a lot that might have required an explanation, but it was more than she could cope with at present to launch into fuller details just to satisfy Jules' curiosity.

'So you are reconciled?' he asked, more puzzled now than startled, his mind seeking the obvious solution to her present attire, or rather lack of it, and Elliott's offensive, dog-with-a-bone attitude.

'Yes!'

'No!' she contradicted Elliott as he gave the answer, shooting him a look of loathing. After his behaviour just now she felt as if she never wanted to set eyes on him again. 'We're still legally tied. But we'll be divorcing as soon as possible.'

'Don't be too sure of that,' he told her furiously.

Jules intervened hastily to stop the full-scale row that might have developed, regardless of his presence there. 'I can see that you still have a lot to discuss,' he suggested, clear on that point at least and anxious to be gone and out of it all. 'And I am decidedly *de trop*. I'll leave you to sort it out between you.'

'Tact as well as a strong sense of self-preservation,' Elliott praised him derisively. 'Perhaps I've underestimated you, Pinot, after all. You should go far with those qualities in the business world.'

'I hope to,' he replied, slightly disconcerted by the remark. He turned to Cassie. 'You have my telephone number if you should need help at all? Ring me if you want someone to talk to.'

She was touched by the offer after the way that she had treated him. 'Thanks, I'll remember,' she said gratefully.

'Cassandra won't be needing any advice from you in the future. She has a husband to turn to now.' Elliott guided the other man firmly to the door.

She sagged with relief at the brief respite and then forced herself to action, snatching up her dress where it had fallen to the floor at the back of the sofa and heading for the bedroom.

'Where do you think you're going?' Elliott demanded angrily, as he came back into the room, his hand snaking out to halt her progress. 'I think it's time for some straight talking, don't you?'

'Possibly,' she said coldly. 'But it'll keep until I've had a shower and got dressed. I can't go home like this.'

'You're not going home. And I prefer you the way that you are at the moment.'

'I've no doubt that you do. But, as I've no intention of consulting your preferences either now or in the distant future, it hardly concerns me what you think.'

She marched past him, shaking off his hand, and went into the bedroom to retrieve the rest of her things. He followed her and when she turned, her arms full of clothes and shoes, he was blocking the doorway. He looked dark and lean and achingly attractive and she had to keep a check on herself not to weaken. Her eyes challenged him to stop her, sparking defiance at him. He shrugged and moved lazily aside.

'Get dressed, if it makes you feel any happier. But

don't think I'll let you walk out of here without getting the truth out of you about your activities since you walked out of my life.'

She gave a short laugh. 'What would you know or care about the truth, Elliott Grant? You twist it to suit your own purposes.' Not waiting for an answer, she went into the bathroom and slammed the door in his face.

For a moment she leaned against it, weak with re-action to the scene she had just been through and ap-prehensive that he might decide to follow her. She would have no power to stop him with no lock on the bathroom door. Not that a locked door would keep him out if he was really determined, she supposed. She heard his footsteps going towards the living room and heaved a sigh of relief. Then, wearily, she went and turned on the taps and, shedding the enveloping folds of the sheet, she stood under the warm, hissing spray, feeling a measure of relief as her body relaxed from the tension of the last few minutes.

She could have stayed there for ever, cocooned from the outside world by the comforting warmth and steam. But she knew perfectly well that Elliott would be im-patient if she didn't reappear soon and it was probably better to face him when he was capable of rational dis-cussion than blinded by anger at her actions. Slowly she towelled herself dry and put on her clothes, grimac-ing at their crumpled lack of freshness.

What a fool she had been to fall for Elliott's tactics of persuasion last night! In a mellow mood induced by the wine and her own willingness to think well of the man she loved, she had genuinely believed all that talk about him settling down on an even keel at last and taking the time to enjoy life's other pleasures besides empire-building. What a gullible little fool he must have thought her to swallow it all! Then it had been a simple matter to overwhelm her last doubts by a skilled assault on her physical vulnerability to him. And she had succumbed without a fight to his lovemaking.

This morning it had meant nothing to him. The cold look of triumph on his face when he had paraded her deliberately in front of Jules had shown her that all too clearly. She wondered bitterly if it had meant anything to him last night. She remembered how eager he had been to get a declaration of her love for him out of her. He had offered her no such assurances and, like an idiot, it had not occurred to her to ask for them. She had thought that his impassioned lovemaking had shown her how he had felt about her. And she had been cruelly mistaken.

She should have remembered that Elliott never liked being bested in anything. Whether he had made her submit to him out of revenge for having the courage to walk out on him and make it clear that she could no longer stand for his idea of marriage, or whether it was more a simple matter of resenting another man's pursuit of what had once been his exclusive property, she did not know. But it hardly mattered why he had done what he had. Only the sickening fact that she had been totally deluded when she imagined that he was still in love with her counted for anything.

The eager happiness of earlier this morning had completely drained away, taking her hopes of a new life for them together with it. Cassie sighed. She felt about ninety, and a glance in the mirror at her tired, drained face and dark-shadowed eyes did nothing to correct the impression. If this was what love did for you, she was having none of it in future. Even her hair seemed to lack its usual bounce and vitality and lay damply against her neck in a heavy, limp mass. She ran a comb through it and then left it; she hadn't the energy to be bothered putting it up.

She sat on the edge of the bath and pondered the position dismally. Elliott had won every point in the game. Was there really any point in fighting against him? She had no notion how she was going to manage to get through his remaining time at the office even if she could dredge up the strength of mind to confront Jules as if he had never witnessed her, flushed and rosy from a night of love with Elliott, clutching the bed linen around her. She went hot at the thought.

'Cassandra!' Elliott's voice came impatiently from the living room. 'If you're not out of there in five seconds flat, I'm coming to fetch you whatever state of undress you're in. Is that clear?'

She did not answer. But he meant what he said, she knew him well enough for that. She got to her feet and headed for the living room with no clear idea in her head of how she would face him. But one thing was certain, she decided, firming her lips purposefully for the scene that awaited her. She might be defeated, but she would go down with her head held high.

CHAPTER TEN

HE was lounging carelessly on the sofa when she went into the room, his long legs stretched out before him and his hands buried in the pockets of his jeans. His expression was enigmatic and she had no way of knowing how he was going to react to her. He glanced up as she entered and patted the padded seat beside him in a silent command. Painfully she remembered how he made the same gesture the night before and how she had gone to sit with him. If she had refused that invitation what a lot of heartache she might have saved herself.

She chose one of the chairs instead and saw his dark brows rise threateningly at the idea that she dared to oppose him still, even in so small a thing. But she had no intention of letting him use the same persuasion upon her that he had employed so successfully last night. 'Well, Elliott,' she said coolly, sitting down and crossing her legs elegantly in front of her. 'What was it that you wanted to talk to me about?'

'I should have thought it was obvious.' He had decided to ignore her gesture of rebellion, probably reckoning that he was better placed where he was to study her reactions and disconcert her with the penetrating gaze to which he subjected her.

'If you mean the little scene in which I was just an unwilling participant, I'd be glad of an explanation.' She forced herself to sound cool and slightly amused, although it was an effort to do so. No doubt a sophisticated woman of the world like Michèle would carry off this sort of thing so much better. But Michèle would know better than to get involved in it in the first place.

'What was it you wanted to know?' Elliott would make a good poker player. He was not giving away anything.

'Well, you could start by telling me exactly what Jules was doing here this morning.'

'I thought I'd already done that. He came to report on yesterday's business trip to Marseilles.'

'Which you fixed up.'

'Which I fixed up,' he agreed. 'I told you, I thought the experience would be good for him. If he wants to get anywhere in the profession he'll have to smarten up his ideas considerably.'

'And I suppose the people you sent along to him to act as clients were paid to create as many problems as possible to ensure that he wouldn't get back until late and come looking for me,' she accused him fiercely. 'You wanted a clear field, didn't you?'

'Yes, I did,' he admitted calmly. 'You didn't think I was capable of it, did you? And I didn't need to pay them for what they did. They were friends of mine.'

She laughed shortly. 'What useful friends you have, Elliott, prepared to tell a pack of lies and give up a free day on your behalf. Would you do the same for them?'

He flushed slightly under his tan. 'If they needed that sort of help. But they don't. And they felt that they owed me a favour.'

'There's no need to make excuses for them,' she flashed. 'Don't worry, I wouldn't expect your friends to be lily-white saints. You're certainly not!'

'The ends occasionally justify the means.'

'And did they in this case?'

His lips firmed tightly. 'I think so.'

'All that effort just to break up whatever you thought Jules and I had going between us?'

'Yes.'

'And was it worth it, Elliott? Do tell me,' she said sweetly. 'I don't expect you to have regrets or feel guilty about what you did. I know that you regard yourself as infallible. But was it really worth all that scheming?'

He studied her bleakly. 'I thought so last night,' he said with deliberation. 'This morning I'm not so sure.'

It was not the answer she expected and for a second or two she was thrown off balance. But she recovered quickly. 'I was glad to hear that you'd enjoyed yourself with me last night,' she said crudely. 'Or was that just another lie thrown at poor Jules to make him jealous because I'd spent the night with you?'

'Oh, you're as skilled as you ever were in that direction. You know how to make a man happy,' he told her. 'You can come to me for a reference any time you need one.'

'I don't think I'll be bothering, thanks.'

'I suppose there are too many others prepared to give you testimonials. Your husband doesn't count for anything. But then I never did, Cassandra, did I?' His eyes were dark with some emotion and for an incredible moment she almost thought there was pain in his expression, before dismissing the idea as fanciful.

'Do you expect me to consider you at all when I know that you're capable of playing tricks like that coldly and deliberately? Why did you do it anyway? Did one night with me mean so much, or was that just an added bonus to the kick it gave you to get rid of my boy-friend for me?'

He was silent and, for once, the man who was never at a loss for a quick answer or a decisive statement seemed to be taking time to consider his next words carefully. 'I don't want it to be for just one night,' he said at last. 'You belong to me, not to Pinot or any other man. I don't care about them. You're *my* wife.'

So that was it. She was right after all. He didn't see her as a person in her own right. She was just one of his possessions that had somehow gone astray and was to be retrieved now that the mood took him. He had been too busy with other things during the last five years to think about her. But now he had decided that the time had come to claim her again. And anyone who got in his way would be ruthlessly dealt with. He had not known that Jules was more friend than lover at this stage. Possibly some time in the future he might have meant more to her, if Elliott had not happened on the scene. But she doubted it somehow. Yet Elliott had not cared what kind of relationship he was breaking up.

'I don't belong to you any more,' she told him. 'You may have decided that you can still find pleasure with me in bed, even if you do despise me, but I'm afraid I'm not interested. You had to have your revenge, didn't you? You found out that I was working for you and you dreamed up a way of getting your own back at me for walking out on you. I suppose your pride must have taken quite a knock.'

There was a tense whiteness about his mouth as if he was having difficulty checking some emotion. For a split second she wondered if he was going to ditch the argument and convince her of his mastery in the way that he had used last night. If he tried to do so he would find her a much less willing partner this time round.

'I want you back, Cassandra,' he said stiffly, as if the words were being forced out of him. 'I need you.'

'*You* need *me*? Don't make me laugh,' she scorned him. 'What exactly do you need me for? Has Michèle suddenly ditched you?'

'I don't want Michèle. After last night I've made my mind up. I want a wife and family. And you're my wife.'

She frowned. 'So you really meant all that last night

about settling down and having children?'

'Is it such a bizarre dream? Surely it's what most people aim for in the end?'

'But you're not "most people", are you, Elliott?' To her his unpredictability had always been one of his most attractive qualities.

'I think I might make a reasonable father, if I worked at it hard enough,' he told her.

She shook her head. 'That's your attitude to everything. You think if you work hard enough, that's all that's needed to give you what you want. But it isn't. You've decided that you want domesticity. I suppose Michèle doesn't like the idea of children. Or perhaps she isn't prepared to wait around for you while you go through the divorce courts. You might change your mind about marrying her when you were free and that would have wasted a lot of valuable time for her. So you're left with the thought that I'll do instead. You eliminate the opposition, get your revenge on me, and graciously take me back as your wife?'

'Perhaps.'

'Well, it won't work. You've wrecked my relationship with Jules and I hope you're proud of it. But he isn't the only man in the world. There'll be others,' she said defiantly, knowing what lies she was offering him as truth, even as she spoke them. 'And if you sack me from McIlroy and Wentworth, I shall be sorry, because I enjoyed working there. But I'll soon find something else to do. I'd rather starve in the street than come back to you!'

He flinched as if she had hit him.

'You can't think of anything in your own defence, can you?' she asked him contemptuously.

'Nothing that would make you listen,' he said wearily. 'No, there's nothing more to say.' There was a defeated look about him that she had never witnessed before and she found it strangely unsettling. She should have been dancing with joy at getting the better of him. Instead, she felt curiously flat, as if the triumph had gone sour on her.

'Only one thing,' she told him, as she picked up her bag and turned to go. 'You forgot the essential ingredient. If you get involved with anyone in the future, I'd advise you to remember that.'

'What is it?' he asked dully.

'Love, Elliott. It must have given you quite a kick to make me tell you that I loved you last night. What an ego trip for you!'

'You didn't mean it?'

'At that point I'd have said anything to keep you with me.' She had to keep her pride intact somehow. She couldn't tell the truth. 'Women are as capable of physical passion as men, you know. But I firmly believe that a marriage needs love to keep it alive. And without love it can't survive, whatever else the two parties have to offer each other in terms of sex or material things. And you don't know what love is,' she told him.

He did not try to stop her as she went to the door and opened it. Then, without a backward glance, she walked out and shut it behind her. In a daze she went down the stairs to the ground floor and made for the door that led to the street. Lost in her unhappiness, she barely noticed the laughing couple who were coming in. But it seemed that one of them knew her and she felt a hand on her arm and heard a friendly voice that was familiar from somewhere saying, 'It's Cassandra, isn't it? Cassandra Grant?'

'Cassandra Russell,' she corrected automatically. She looked up to see before her the features of a blonde who, although they had never met officially, was all too familiar to her. It was the woman who had been at Elliott's flat all that time ago when she had called to make an effort to mend the differences between herself and Elliott.

'You're Liz,' she said stupidly.

'That's right. And this is my husband, Peter.'

Dimly Cassie registered a tall, bearded man, about the same age as Elliott, who was smiling at her. She muttered something, she hardly knew what, in his direction.

'We were just going to see Elliott.' The woman called Liz sounded anxious. 'I don't want to seem interfering, but is it—that is—is everything sorted out between you now?'

'Yes, thank you,' Cassie replied politely, and suddenly the tears were streaming uncontrollably down her face. 'I'm sorry,' she gulped, and groped for a handkerchief.

She felt the man thrust one into her hand and she used it gratefully. She was dimly aware of a whispered conversation between them and then she heard Liz's voice suggesting, 'Look, you need a stiff drink or a cup of coffee or something. There's a little bar down the road. We'll take you there.' She did not suggest going back to Elliott's flat, for which Cassie felt only relief.

She allowed them to steer her in the direction of the café and sit her down at a little table there. Mercifully, at this time in the morning, it was nearly empty and there was hardly anyone to comment on the spectacle of a tear-stained English girl frantically mopping away at her eyes in an effort to regain some semblance of calm.

Peter disappeared to order the drinks and Liz patted her arm comfortingly, enquiring, 'Do you feel a little better now?'

Cassie gave a shaky laugh. 'Thanks. I don't know what came over me. I don't usually burst into tears on complete strangers!'

The other girl eyed her seriously. 'But we're not complete strangers, are we? We met that day at the flat when you came back to see Elliott.'

Cassie nodded. 'Yes. He called you Liz. That's why I remembered.'

'I've felt guilty about that ever since. That's why when Elliott told us that he was going to——' She broke off as Peter returned with the drinks.

'I didn't know if you'd prefer coffee or something stronger,' he said with a smile. 'So I brought both for all of us. I think we probably need it.'

He pushed a small cognac towards Cassie with instructions to drink it at once and she obeyed him. She certainly needed it, and the cool liquid that burnt a fiery path down her throat certainly restored her to a degree of normality.

'Good,' said Liz firmly, when she admitted as much to her. 'Because we've got a lot to tell you.'

'About you and Elliott?' Cassie glanced at Peter, but he did not seem to be surprised by the way she coupled the names. Perhaps the other girl had confessed everything to him. Or could it all have happened before he came on the scene?

'Yes.' Liz paused, clearly working out where to begin, and then shrugged and launched straight into the tale. 'You remember that day when you came round and caught me in—well, what you obviously thought were guilty circumstances?'

'Yes?' She could hardly forget it.

'I know it looked bad, but in fact it was quite innocent. Peter was with me at the time, but you didn't see him.'

'Begin at the beginning, love. You're confusing her,' her husband said.

She pulled a face at him and did as instructed. 'I expect Elliott told you about his early life in the child-

ren's home? Well, that was where I first met him. I
was nine years old and a bit of a problem child. I'd
been put out for fostering, but it had gone wrong for
various reasons and I was getting a bit old for adoption.
Would-be parents are usually looking for an attractive
baby or a toddler. It takes a bit of doing to saddle yourself with a nine-year-old who's not particularly good-
looking and has a record of making herself disagreeable
in foster-homes. Elliott wasn't eligible for adoption
either.'

'I know,' said Cassie quickly. 'His mother wouldn't
let him go.'

'He was a little older than I was, but we had a lot in
common. We were both crying out for a bit of love and
stability. And I think we probably found it in each
other. We always vowed that we'd keep in touch when
we'd left the home and we did in a sporadic sort of way.
I'm not terribly good at writing letters and Elliott was
busy getting ahead. Then I had a letter from him, saying that he'd met the only girl in the world for him and
had married her.'

'He didn't invite you to the wedding?' Cassie was
puzzled.

'No. I was away nursing in Singapore at the time, so
there wouldn't have been any point. But Elliott told
me that the very next time I was in London I was to
call and he'd introduce us.'

'He never mentioned you.'

'I expect he had other things on his mind,' Liz
laughed. 'From what he told me, he was too stuck
on you to be even thinking about anything else. He
sounded on Cloud Nine. In the meantime I'd got
equally interesting news for him.' She glanced across
the table at Peter and smiled. It was obvious to Cassie
that she was devoted to him. 'Peter was working as a
doctor in Singapore and we got together and realised

that we were right for each other. We got married quickly out there and took our first leave home as our honeymoon. We thought that we'd surprise you both by calling to break the news and perhaps stay for a while and get to know you. I'd told Peter a lot about Elliott.'

The slow light was beginning to dawn on Cassie and she had a suspicion of what was coming next.

'Elliott was pleased to see us,' Liz went on. 'But I could tell that there was something badly wrong. Finally I dragged it out of him about your quarrel and how you'd left him. He was shattered. It took quite a bit of talking to him to boost his ego and reassure him that there was still a chance for him if he made the right moves.'

'Elliott? Elliott needed reassurance?' Cassie could hardly credit it.

Liz gave her a sharp look. 'He may give the impression that he's invulnerable and I expect it's true in business. But where his emotions are concerned he tends to see hurts and rejection even when they aren't there.'

'But he hadn't exactly lived like a monk, when I met him,' Cassie protested.

'Oh, there were lots of women in his life. But he loved them and left them fairly callously. He never got involved, although they quite often fell for him. But you were different.'

'I see.'

'When you walked out on him, he didn't know what to do for the first time in his life.'

Peter took up the story. 'He insisted that we stay at the flat and wouldn't hear of it when we suggested going to a hotel. He turned out of his room so that we could have it and he slept in the spare room because it only had a single bed.'

'So, when I saw Liz going into that bedroom——'

'You naturally assumed the worst,' Peter completed for her. 'We were getting ready to go out, actually.'

Cassie sat stunned. 'But it all seemed so damning,' she said. 'And Elliott never explained.'

'You didn't give him a chance, did you?' Liz pointed out. 'And afterwards, when he tried to get in touch with you, his letters were sent back unopened and you wouldn't take his phone calls. A man has his pride, and Elliott's got more than most.'

'Letters? Phone calls?' She was puzzled. 'I didn't know there'd been any.' She had a sudden flash of understanding. No doubt her mother had discreetly ensured that she didn't hear about them. Elliott's feelings of antipathy for her mother had been returned with interest by Mrs Russell. She had made no secret of her joy about the marriage break-up.

'It sounds as if you got your wires properly crossed,' Liz told her. 'He tried everything. But when you didn't get in touch, he could only assume that you didn't care any more, and he stopped making the effort. He just buried himself in his work.' She frowned. 'We were worried about him. We were back in England by that time and we didn't live that far away from him, so we were able at least to keep an eye on him.'

'He must have had girl-friends.'

'Nothing serious. We had the feeling that he hadn't got over you, although,' the other girl looked slightly embarrassed, 'we kept telling him that you weren't worth it. When he heard that there was a Cassandra Russell working for one of the branch offices he'd acquired when he took over Prospect Properties, nothing would satisfy him until he'd found out beyond the shadow of a doubt whether it was you. He came round to us and told us that he was going to visit the office on some excuse and see how the land lay. We'd planned to come out here on holiday anyway, so we offered to help if we could.'

'So it was you two who went with Jules to Marseilles?'

'Yes. I'm afraid we led him a merry dance too,' Peter chuckled. 'We'd been told to keep him out of the way to give Elliott a chance to talk to you, and we did just that.'

'Elliott had some plan to get you back to him,' Liz explained. 'He didn't give us any details. I—I gather it misfired.'

Cassie smiled bitterly. 'You could say that. If only I'd known that he cared so much. He never told me.' She gave them a brief, censored résumé, ending by telling them, 'I'd have done or said anything to hurt him. And I'm very much afraid that I did.'

'And now?' Liz asked gently. 'What are you going to do about it?'

'There's only one thing I can do, isn't there? I'll go back and try to sort things out.' Cassie sighed. 'We both said some terrible things. I just hope that it's not too late.'

Liz gave her hand a comforting squeeze. 'I'm sure it won't be if you really want to put things right.' She grinned. 'We'll stay here and sample the local vino, shall we, Pete?'

'We'll drink to Elliott's return to married life,' he agreed.

In spite of their encouragement Cassie felt desperately anxious as she climbed the stairs to Elliott's flat and rang the bell. She had played this scene before, with disastrous results.

It was a while before he answered and she wondered, terrified, if he had gone out. What if he had decided to find solace with Michèle? Peter and Liz had not mentioned her. Then the door opened and Elliott stood there looking at her as if she was a ghost.

She licked her dry, nervous lips. 'Can I come in?'

For a second she thought he was going to refuse. Then, without a word, he stood back and let her go past him into the flat. She went into the living room and stood there clutching her bag to her and wondering where to start on the explanations. He followed her and leaned against the doorjamb, studying her warily through narrowed eyes.

'You've been crying,' he said roughly.

'Yes.' There was no point denying it, with red-rimmed eyes and a tear-stained face.

'Over Jules? Did it mean that much to you?'

'No. He didn't mean anything to me.' She watched him carefully for a reaction, but he was giving nothing away.

'I see,' he said, and that was all.

'I met your friends, Liz and Peter.' She tried again, hoping desperately for some encouragement from him. 'They're in a bar down the road. They told me——'

'What?' The question came at her like a bullet.

She braced herself and decided to try shock tactics. 'They told me you were in love with me.'

'I was.'

It was not an easy response to follow up, but she could not fail now. It mustn't be too late for them. 'What about now?' she asked.

'No,' he said uncompromisingly. 'I told you that a while back.'

'Oh, I see.' She had killed what there was between them with her foolish behaviour. He didn't care any more. The hot tears fell and spilled down her cheeks and she brushed at them angrily. What must he be thinking?

'For God's sake, Cassandra, what are you trying to do to me?' Suddenly he was at her side, removing her bag roughly from her nerveless grip and taking her in his arms as if he would never let her go.

'Oh, Elliott, I love you. I love you so,' she sobbed.

He held her close to him. 'Do you think I don't love you almost to the edge of madness?'

His words penetrated her tired brain and she raised a tear-drenched face to his. 'But you said——'

'I was splitting hairs to save my pride,' he told her. 'I said I wasn't *in* love with you any more. I suppose it's true, really. What I felt for you before, when we were just married, was an idealistic sort of feeling. I'd met lots of women and enjoyed myself with them, even fancied myself in love with a couple of them. But when I met you I knew that they'd meant nothing to me. You knocked me for six.'

She smiled shakily. 'You had the same effect on me. You still do.'

'I was in love with you, sure, but I didn't love you enough to care about making you happy. I wasn't prepared to compromise. I wanted it all my way, didn't I? And, in my selfish, pig-headed way, I assumed that you'd be glad to give in to me.'

'It must have been quite a shock to you when I didn't.'

He nodded. 'I knew that you had a mind of your own, but it never occurred to me that you'd stand up to me the way you did. I was blazing mad.'

He lifted her in his arms and carried her to the sofa. 'We've been a pair of fools,' he admitted as he kissed her. Her arms wound round him as she returned the embrace, disappointed when he broke away from her.

He smiled down and at her and she thought how little she had seen of that softened look on his face during the last weeks. How different his stern features looked when he relaxed! 'Explanations first, Cassandra, or we'll get involved with other things and I'll never hear them.'

She raised her lips invitingly to his. 'Are you sure you really want to hear them?' she asked him enticingly.

'Very much.' But he dragged his gaze reluctantly away.

She leant back happily against him. 'All that matters is that I love you and I nearly lost you a second time round because I was too proud to tell you. I thought you didn't care for me, Elliott. I thought that you'd fallen for Michèle.'

He looked faintly amused. 'At least some of my schemes worked, then. I meant you to think that, you little fool.'

'And you didn't?'

'Michèle Durand is a very attractive woman, who needs a husband to keep her in order,' he said. 'Because, if he doesn't, she'll walk all over him. But I'm not the man to do it and I've indicated as much to her. I'm afraid I couldn't raise enough interest in the lady.'

'But she's beautiful and sophisticated and——'

'And cold and hard and calculating,' he finished the list for her. 'All admirable qualities, I'm sure. But not in *my* wife.'

'Really?'

'Do you need convincing that I prefer your charms any day?' He bent his head to hers again and for a few moments neither of them said anything. He was breathing hard when he let her go.

'I was so jealous of her,' Cassie admitted.

'*You* were jealous? *I* wanted to tear Pinot limb from limb when I saw him holding your hand across the table at the Belle Madeleine. Be glad that I didn't.'

'No. You took it out on me instead.'

'Can you blame me?'

She shook her head. 'I suppose I was trying to make you jealous too. I kept telling myself that I hated you and I wanted to show you that I didn't care.'

'And you made a pretty good job of it,' he told her. 'You nearly drove me mad. I kept thinking about the other men who'd shared your life and your bed, while I was left out in the cold, rejected.' His eyes were suddenly bleak with the memory. 'I was obsessed with you. When I first came out here I had some crazy idea at the back of my mind for getting my own back on you. I wanted you back, but you had to pay for what you'd made me suffer first. But that all went out of my head the first time I saw you. I knew then that I didn't care what had happened between us. I just had to have you back on any terms. But you weren't interested, were you?'

She nuzzled up to him. 'I would have been, if you'd told me that instead of acting like a bear with a sore head all the time.'

He shrugged. 'I was furious. Then I realised that however indifferent you claimed that you were to me, I could still turn you on physically. I could tell that the first time I kissed you.'

'Yes,' she admitted. 'But I tried not to respond.'

'I hoped that it might be some kind of basis for us to get back together. I wanted you back on any level.'

'So you decided that you'd start by eliminating the opposition?'

'Can you blame me?'

She shook her head. 'I suppose not. You did tell me all was fair in love and war. But he didn't get anywhere with me, Elliott. Lots of men have fancied their chances with me since I left you. But the memory of what I shared with you broke it up every time.'

He pulled her closer to him. 'And your image came between me and every woman I took out in an effort to forget you.'

'I'll try never to make you jealous again,' she promised.

He gave a confident smile. 'You won't be given the chance to try.'

'Mm.' Suddenly she remembered something that Liz had told her, and turned to him, eager to tell him. 'Elliott, I never knew that you'd written to me. My mother——'

His lips firmed angrily. 'I should have guessed she'd had something to do with it.'

'She didn't like you very much.'

'She resented me for taking you away from her,' he said briefly. 'But I'm afraid she's going to have to get used to it second time round.' And then his mouth came down on hers again and those were the last words that he spoke to her for some considerable time.

Guiltily Cassie came back to earth from a long, shattering kiss and remembered Liz and Peter. 'They'll be waiting for us, Elliott. They'll be wondering what happened,' she told him.

'I think they'll have guessed by now,' he said. 'And if they haven't, they'll just have to wait a while longer before their curiosity's satisfied. We've got a lot of catching up to do.'

'But, Elliott——'

He kissed her again. 'Any objections?' he asked, raising a dark brow.

'No,' she said.

And, lifting her up, he carried her purposefully into the next room.

The Mills & Boon Rose is the Rose of Romance

Every month there are ten new titles to choose from — ten new stories about people falling in love, people you want to read about, people in exciting, far away places. Choose Mills & Boon. It's your way of relaxing.

December's titles are:

TEMPLE OF THE DAWN by *Anne Hampson*
Lexa lost her heart to Paul Mansell — but his heart belonged, as it always would, to his beautiful dead wife Sally . . .

MY DARLING SPITFIRE by *Rosemary Carter*
The only way Siane could join her fiancé on a remote game reserve was to go in the company of the *maddening* André Connors!

KONA WINDS by *Janet Dailey*
Happy in her teaching job in Hawaii, Julie then met her pupil's grim half-brother . . .

BOOMERANG BRIDE by *Margaret Pargeter*
Four years ago, when Vicki was expecting her husband Wade's child, he had thrown her out. So why was he now forcing her to return?

SAVAGE INTERLUDE by *Carole Mortimer*
James St Just was Kate's half-brother, but Damien Savage didn't know that, and he had jumped to all the wrong conclusions . . .

THE JASMINE BRIDE by *Daphne Clair*
Rachel didn't think it mattered that she was so much younger than Damon Curtis — but she was also very much more inexperienced . . .

CHAMPAGNE SPRING by *Margaret Rome*
The arrogant Marquis de la Roque thought the worst of Chantal and her brother — but she was determined to prove him wrong!

DEVIL ON HORSEBACK by *Elizabeth Graham*
Joanne went as housekeeper to Alex Harper — but he was convinced that she was only yet another candidate for the position of his wife . . .

PRINCE OF DARKNESS by *Susanna Firth*
After five years' separation from her husband Elliott, Cassie was just about getting over it when Elliott turned up again — as her boss.

COUNTRY COUSIN by *Jacqueline Gilbert*
Eleanor liked most of the Mansel family. What a pity she couldn't feel the same way about one of them, the uncompromising Edward . . .

If you have difficulty in obtaining any of these books from your local paperback retailer, write to:

Mills and Boon Reader Service
P.O. Box No 236, Thornton Road, Croydon, Surrey CR9 3RU.

Doctor Nurse Romances

December's
stories of romantic relationships behind the scenes
of modern medical life are:

A ROSE FOR THE SURGEON
by Lisa Cooper

Was it Doctor Rob Delaney, who had once broken
Sister Anna's heart, who had sent her red roses? And
if not, who had?

THE DOCTOR'S CHOICE
by Hilary Wilde

Nurse Claire Butler had been brutally jilted. How
could she trust any other man — let alone the one
who had warned her not to fall in love on the rebound?

Order your copies today from your local paperback retailer.

Masquerade
Historical Romances

Intrigue
excitement
romance

THE SHADOW QUEEN
by Margaret Hope

It was Kirsty's uncanny — and potentially dangerous — resemblance to Mary, Queen of Scots, that saved her from an arranged marriage with Dirk Farr, the gipsy laird. But had she only exchanged one peril for another?

ROSAMUND
by Julia Murray

Sir Hugh Eavleigh could not forget Rose, the enchanting waif who had tried to rob him on the King's Highway. Then he learned that she was really Lady Rosamund Daviot — his prospective bride!

Look out for these titles in your local paperback shop from 14th December 1979

191

ORDER NOW FOR DIRECT DELIVERY

Choose from this selection of

Mills & Boon FAVOURITES
— ALL HIGHLY RECOMMENDED

☐ C211
THIS MOMENT IN TIME
Lilian Peake

☐ C212
PETALS DRIFTING
Anne Hampson

☐ C213
THE NIGHT OF THE BULLS
Anne Mather

☐ C214
THREE WEEKS IN EDEN
Anne Weale

☐ C215
HUNTER OF THE EAST
Anne Hampson

☐ C216
TIME OF CURTAINFALL
(Darling Rhadamanthus)
Margery Hilton

☐ C217
BAUHINIA JUNCTION
Margaret Way

☐ C218
DESERT DOCTOR
Violet Winspear

☐ C219
DARK ENEMY
Anne Mather

☐ C220
MY HEART'S A DANCER
Roberta Leigh

☐ C221
SECRET HEIRESS
Eleanor Farnes

☐ C222
THE PAGAN ISLAND
Violet Winspear

☐ C223
JAKE HOWARD'S WIFE
Anne Mather

☐ C224
A GIRL ALONE
Lilian Peake

☐ C225
WHISPERING PALMS
Rosalind Brett

☐ C226
A QUESTION OF MARRIAGE
Rachel Lindsay

ONLY 55p EACH

SIMPLY TICK ☑ YOUR SELECTION(S) ABOVE THEN JUST COMPLETE AND POST THE ORDER FORM OVERLEAF ▶